CONVENIENCE

*Copyright © 2017 Chrome Valley Books
All rights reserved.*

Convenience

Written by Andrew Mackay

Edited by Nessie Braeburn

Cover design by Kreacher

ISBN: 9781973219743
Copyright © 2017 Chrome Valley Books

This is a work of fiction. Names, characters, places and incidents either are products of the author's imagination or are used fictitiously. Any resemblance to actual persons, living or dead (or somewhere in between), events, or locales is entirely coincidental.

No part of this book may be reproduced in any form or by any electronic or mechanical means including information storage and retrieval systems, without permission in writing from the author. The only exception is by a reviewer who may quote short excerpts in a review.

Chapters

Chapter 1 *08:50 – 10:00* 1

Chapter 2 *10:00 – 11:00* 25

Chapter 3 *11:00 – 12:00* 49

Chapter 4 *12:00 – 13:00* 71

Chapter 5 *13:00 – 14:00* 93

Chapter 6 *14:00 – 15:00* 109

Chapter 7 *15:00 – 16:00* 127

Chapter 8 *16:00 – 17:00* 141

Chapter 9 *17:00 – 18:00* 163

Acknowledgements *188*

Get Your Free Short Horror Story! *188*

About the author *191*

Chapter 1
08:50 – 10:00

Drip, drip, drip…

Even now I can hear it. That incessant, repetitive sound of water hitting the floor. It won't stop. There's a certain rhythm to it that makes me think of my father. Well, not the actual person but, rather, a music track that reminds me of him.

He passed away twenty-odd years ago.

The way the droplets attack the hard floor. The rhythm reminds me of the chorus of *Save Your Kisses For Me* by The Brotherhood of Man. A tune my son used to love.

As I lay awake in bed right now I can't get the tune out of my head. But it's not the tune, you see. It's the drip, drip, dripping. I haven't checked my bedside clock yet, but my intuition tells me it's around half past three in the morning.

There's no-one next to me in my double bed. Not anymore. I've grown used to the fact that she's no longer there.

Tossing and turning in bed doesn't help me get to sleep. I've been up since five in the morning, and it's nearly twenty-four hours later.

I have to be at work at eight-thirty. Why can't I get to sleep? I remember someone once advised me that I should clear my head of everything possible. Make a mental diagram of every muscle and organ in my body. Visualize it on the ceiling, and go around them - one by one - forcing them to relax. "Sink into the mattress" is what I *think* I was told.

Imagine nothing.

I've spent the past hour at least doing this to no avail. My muscles and shoulders are perfectly relaxed.

I just wish I could fall asleep.

***

8:50 am on a Thursday morning. The *Kaleidoscope Shopping Mall* in *Chrome Valley* wasn't populated with shoppers.

Not yet, anyway.

The shopping center staff are all busy, though. Especially the cleaners. Giant industrial vacuums are tugged along by portly workers. They dance their merry way up both levels of the mall. They pick up discarded packets of food. Autumnal leaves that have been trodden in by shoppers from the road outside. Also, many discarded items are left haphazardly on the ground.

A broken umbrella.

A half-empty packet of tampons.

A discarded milkshake. Its contents splattered in every direction across the ground.

One of them even found a wallet with twenty pounds in it. The wallet in question had been returned safe and sound to the information desk. Slap-bang in the middle of the lower level hall. The money wasn't inside it when the customer came to pick it up a few minutes ago.

The assistant claimed it was how she found it. The customer didn't believe her and so kicked up a bit of a fuss, accusing the assistant of thievery.

The assistant refused to cave in. She stood her ground, claiming that the item had been handed in by a cleaner before her shift started. Once it had been identified by the customer (it had a fluffy monkey attached to it - the item, not the customer) she had simply presented the owner with it.

A complaint was sure to follow. Not so much as a thank you.

On the first level, just by the south area's spiral staircase, a cleaner was using her vacuum. The device sucked up a patch of *something*. It might have been crumbs from a sandwich. Maybe it was the stony remnants of a bucket of popcorn discarded by a cinema-goer in the small hours on their way to the car park.

What the cleaner hadn't accounted for was the electric cord snaking a few inches away from her feet.

Thirty-six seconds earlier, the customer who'd complained about his wallet made his way up the very same stairs. He'd noticed the cord and stepped over it, causing the cleaner to smile at him and step sideways.

The two events led to the cord becoming taut between the wall socket and the cylindrical vacuum. The cord hung approximately eight inches up from the floor. A dastardly tripwire for any oncoming pedestrian.

Because the cleaner was lost in her own world listening to music via her earphones, she wasn't as alert as she might have been.

Her heel jabbed into the cord. She didn't notice it happening. She *did* notice when she tried to regain her composure with her other foot. The ceiling of the Kaleidoscope shopping mall barrel-rolled around her, indicating that she'd tripped.

The back of her head slammed against the tiled ground, knocking her out.

The vacuum continued to whir.

Worse still, in the age of perpetual CCTV and heightened security, no-one came to her aid. None of the security guards were around.

She lay there, silent - the music playing in her ears. The vacuum continued to roar away.

The blood slowly pooled around her head as she lay unconscious.

"Five minutes till doors open," came a friendly female voice through the speaker address system. Nobody was around. The echo of the announcement rattled through the walls like a stampeding herd of elephants.

Dressed in his overalls and trainers, Will Gee looked up from the service entrance to the south perimeter. He'd heard the announcement.

He wasn't an especially quick man, all told. Willy was in his fifties and seemed for all the world like the life had been sucked right out of him. He blinked at the glass ceiling that promised a bright and sunny day and tried to smile. But he couldn't.

This morning, Willy's eyes were a reddish purple. This was a man who'd not managed to sleep much during the night. He looked down at his right arm and lifted it. Again, the motion was very slow. A plaster hugged over the webbing between his thumb and index finger. Some blood had managed to seep through, but the dressing would surely hold for a few hours yet.

Blink, blink...

The haze of the roaring sun wafted over the glass ceiling. That yucky stingy sensation of a night of no sleep crept across his cornea. He blinked a few more times, hoping his eyelids would windscreen-wiper away the damp.

"Hey, Willy," the assistant yelled. She offered smile and waved at him.

Willy turned around and looked at her. Beautiful red lips and a waterfall of beautiful blond hair falling down her back. She was the perfect front-of-house for the wonders of the *Kaleidoscope Shopping Mall.*

Maybe one day he'd find out her name. She worked on Thursdays and Fridays. Willy's place of work was in the southern part of the shopping mall. It meant that he'd need to walk for approximately three minutes to the information desk.

She clocked something may not be going right with his

day, "You okay, Willy?"

He turned to the staircase and nodded up at the second-to-last step. The cleaner was still passed out from her fall.

The assistant opened the service hatch and walked over to where he was standing.

Clomp, clomp, clomp… the heels of her shoes seemed to "ping" like an aggressive cash register with each step. "What is it, Willy?"

Once again, he nodded at the top of the stairs. She took a look, now that she had an adequate view of the spiral.

"Oh, my God. She's fallen."

The blonde assistant hightailed it up at the dozens of twisty-turny steps as fast as her pretty little heels could carry her. She reached the cleaner and crouched to her knees.

She snapped her fingers, attempting to catch the cleaner's attention, "Hello? Can you hear me?"

"Willy, can you call security—" the assistant tutted to herself and removed the woman's earphones.

She turned around to find that Willy had gone.

***

"Store opening in two minutes," the speaker system advised as Willy made his way past the shops.

Right now everything was clean. The floors were so shiny you can just about make out every detail of your contouring as you walked.

Willy was a slow walker. At his age, the job he had was taking its toll. It was the work of an outright contortionist at times. Bending over forwards, backwards, left and right. He spent many months of his life on his knees fixing pipework. At other times, he cleaned up a whole host of nastiness from the floors.

He sauntered past the twenty-foot lantern that stood

proudly in the middle of the shops. The flame burned brightly. It was unclear what its actual purpose was. God alone knew what it supposedly advertised, or what it meant to symbolize.

A new store had opened named *TriMarque*. It sold cheap clothing, most of it imported from China and other faraway places. On the day of its opening back in February, there were protesters outside claiming that the store was operating unethically. Rumor had it that it did business with firms that used child labor.

It didn't seem to stop the store flourishing, though. It was a ten-second walk from the corridor that leads to the public restrooms. In about two minutes' time, the place would be heaving with shoppers looking for today's bargain.

The woman working there unbolted the double doors and smiled at Willy as he walked past. She'd seen him a few times over the months she'd started working there. To Willy, she was just another faceless, listless retailer.

He wasn't looking at her through the windowed door as she smiled. He was looking at his own reflection.

Willy had heard from many of the frequenters of this shopping mall that clothing stores installed warped mirrors in their changing rooms. They did it so that prospective buyers looked good when they tried on the garments. It seemed to work.

As Willy paused to check his reflection in the window he, too, seemed to have slimmed down over the past weeks and months. He pressed his palms to his belly. His overalls creased out.

From portly and ungainly to scarily thin in such a small amount of time. It wasn't a sight anyone would want to commit to memory. Willy continued to walk toward his place of work.

He walked past the *Bean There, Done That* coffee shop. The store stood on the corner of the lower level main thoroughfare and the southern perimeter walkway.

The coffee shop would also be heaving with customers. At this time in the morning, they'd grab themselves a quick *Crappycino* before making their way to the train station. Or their offices at the center. It wasn't a place Willy would have ever visited. He had a packed lunch in his right hand and a flask in his left.

The stench of freshly-brewed coffee did at least sweep away the pungent aroma coming from the public restrooms, though.

Bean There, Done That looked scarily empty. A lone light behind the service counter lit up the sandwiches behind the glass panel. There didn't appear to be any staff members milling around.

And then...

The door flew open, revealing a skinny man named Jeffrey in his brown uniform. It made Willy jump in his shoes.

"Hey man, you okay?" Jeffrey asked. His shiny name badge on his lapel reflected the light across Willy's tired eyes.

Willy held his chest and nodded, letting out a little cough.

"Gonna be a busy today, isn't it?" he asked as he kicked out a folding stand with the side of his shoe. He unclipped the metal and folded out the advertisement that stood by the window. A free muffin when you buy a large coffee until midday.

"I gotta say, though," Jeffrey continued. "I don't envy you. Having to put up with all that piss and shit all day."

Willy looked down at his shoes and half-smiled.

"You get fed up with the smell of coffee beans, but you get used to it. I dunno how you can put up with the stench of bleach and feces—"

Willy walked off. He was completely uninterested in what Jeffrey had to say. To him, he was just another lifeless clone. Much like all of the workers who spent the day in any of the one hundred and eighteen stores that were ensconced within the *Kaleidoscope*.

Willy began his journey down the fifty-foot-long walkway. The path shot out of the mall like a mad artery leading to nowhere.

It was a journey he'd taken at least ten thousand times since the mall opened thirty years ago.

Exactly seven equidistant bulbs ran along the ceiling separated out by a quad of sixteen tiles. The third and sixth bulb didn't work properly and flickered on and off. Actually, it wasn't so much on and off as "whatever random act it felt like doing."

The result made the walkway dank and depressing, like the queue for a horror train at a theme park.

A pink elephant with a blue saddle marked the halfway point. Made of plastic, it was a children's ride that offered the occupant a decidedly dodgy to-and-fro for the nominal sum of fifty pence per go. It was surprisingly popular when the schools were done for the day.

When a kid stopped their parent en route to the toilets, they'd demand to ride the pink elephant. Every time their demands were met, you'd know about it.

Willy didn't want to think about that as he reached into his pocket and took out his bunch of keys. He half-entertained the notion of stopping at the drinks dispenser. The prospect of an overpriced cola was inviting but, eventually, he thought better of it. He had a tin of drink in his lunch box.

Perhaps he could make it last all day. Besides, one pound fifty for a small bottle of cola was a bloody rip-off.

The convenience area outside the toilets was bulbous. That is to say, if the walkway there was the shaft of the penis, then the bathrooms were the base.

A gentleman's facility loomed to the right acting as the southern-most *testicle*. The one to the left was the ladies. The middle unit, fondly referred to as *the perineum*, housed the baby changing facilities.

Opposite all three was the janitor's office. Willy Gee's place of work.

He threw the gold key into the lock and turned it.

The door flung inward and allowed him inside. He set his lunch box onto the wooden computer desk that faced the door. Willy shook the flask and unscrewed the cap. He held it in his hand and poured some of the piping hot contents into it.

Sip, sip, sip.

Ahhh. *Mostly* fresh coffee. Perhaps the one part of the day that'd be worth living for.

Willy closed his eyes for a few seconds. He knew any moment now that the piped-in muzak would begin to play.

Sure enough, it did. Like clockwork.

A tinny mock-jazz version of *Sweet Child O' Mine* by Guns & Roses spat out through the decades-old speakers. It was pathetic. If anyone were to scramble toward the toilet with their trousers around their ankles, they'd be losing weight to Axl Rose's dulcet tones.

Willy sniggered to himself and opened his eyes. It was past nine in the morning, now.

A picture of him and his family stood on the corner of the desktop. He swallowed down his mouthful of coffee and stared at it in something of a daze. It didn't last long. He'd had enough and returned to the vacated section of his brain, trying to settle on his duties for the day.

The ladies and gents needed unlocking and made available for the punters.

He threw the metal key ring over his middle finger and swung them around his hand.

With absolute precision, one gold key with a pink cover fell between his index and middle finger.

The flask lid hit the desk and Will walked out of the office.

The pink-headed key ran out from the keyhole. Willy stepped inside the ladies toilet and performed a quick scan. Sheila, his colleague, had cleaned up before she clocked off last night. It would appear that she'd done a very good job.

The row of six washbasins was in pristine order. Each mirror had been squeegeed to near-perfection. It was almost as if you could eat your dinner off it.

Opposite the basins, all six cubicle doors were all half-open. They seemed to offer the potential occupier to come in and relieve themselves.

Each toilet roll holder was fully stocked, with a secondary roll of paper housed in the plastic compartment.

The seats were all clean and the floors were immaculate.

There was just one thing missing this morning.

Sheila.

Willy walked out of the ladies toilet and into the convenience area. He took out his phone and hit the screen.

As he waited for Sheila to answer, a woman made her way toward him from the corridor.

"Oh. Excuse me," the woman said, "Do you work here?"

Willy nodded and kept the phone to his ear.

"Oh. Thank God for that," she hitched her skirt up and ran into the ladies toilet.

"Hi, this is Sheila," came a voice from Willy's phone. "I can't get to the phone right now. Please leave a—"

Willy cut the call and immediately redialed. He took a seat on the waiting bench, crossed his legs and jangled a bunch of keys in his free hand.

"Hi, this is Sheila. I can't—"

Willy cut the call one again. As he passed the phone to his other hand, he felt something knock against the side of his shoe.

He looked down to find a nasty little rat looking up at him with an apologetic face.

Willy scowled and shooed it away with his foot. The furry creature scuttled away under the bench.

He lowered himself to his knees and pressed his hands onto the edge of the bench. His eyes moved under the wood and spotted a scared, little creature huffing back at him.

Its face indicated that it didn't want any trouble and was simply lost.

Willy clicked his fingers and urged it toward him. He wasn't going to do it any harm. Neither were to blame for the rat being there. That particular accusation could be levelled at the coffee shop for refusing to dispose of their waste properly.

Click, click. Willy snapped his fingers.

The rat refused to move. It moved back on its haunches, against the skirting board.

Willy moved in.

"Oh. My God," a woman screamed from the door, "What on Earth do you think you're doing?"

Willy banged his head on the underside of the bench. He gripped the edge and pulled his head out from under it. Shock and surprise fell across his face.

The woman adjusted her waist as the door to the ladies swung shut behind her.

"Were you looking up my skirt?" She was deadly serious asking that question.

Willy shook his head in defiance.

"Filthy pervert. I should report you."

Willy rose to his feet and held out his hands. He was about to speak, but the young woman was *so* offended.

"Ugh, no," she stormed off in a temper, "I don't wanna hear it. Your type make me sick."

Clomp, clomp, clomp.

As the Guns N Roses track came to an abrupt end, so, too, did Willy's time with the woman who had figured him out wrong.

It made him chuckle. He had stories galore of mishaps

and misunderstandings during his time working here. This morning's first customer would be one for the record books. It'd make for an entertaining story for his friends down the pub later. Or, at least it would if he had any friends.

Willy looked down at his shoe. The rat stood beside him, almost assuming its position as an ally.

Willy chuckled at it as it looked up at him. Maybe the pair could laugh about this one day. The furry little bastard was about as close a friend as Willy had these days.

The gents toilet.

Willy had a hospital appointment early yesterday evening. He hadn't cleaned up quite as thoroughly as he'd have liked. It wasn't a bad job, though.

Much like in the ladies toilet, the basins were all clean, here. They weren't immaculate. Even if they had been, the first hour of business would have rendered it looking as it was. Acceptable. The odd pubic hair lined the ceramic. Spots of red stuff could be removed with a thorough scrub.

The gents layout was the mirror opposite to the ladies in every respect. Six basins, six cubicles, six urinals.

The sixth urinal at the end of the bank was knee-height for visitors who were of a certain age or disposition. The cubicles sat right next to them.

The first five were like the basins. Acceptable.

Willy knew that the sixth cubicle was problematic and kept it locked from the outside. Some comedian had barged past Willy as he was locking up for the night yesterday. He claimed it was a life or death situation.

Willy remembered looking at his watch and suggesting he try elsewhere. The cinema on the same level had facilities available, but the gentleman wouldn't hear of it.

He barged past and helped himself to the cubicle furthest away and let rip.

In retrospect, Willy forgave the man his ill-founded

behavior. After all, no-one *wants* to inconvenience the staff for the sake of a joke. Judging by the sound of turmoil coming from the cubicle, it seemed that the urgency was genuine.

After the man emptied his bowels and ran off, Willy had a cursory glance of the contents of the bowl. He wasn't curious as to what had happened. A simple check that everything was in order needed to happen. Once that was over, he could lock up for the night.

It wasn't what he'd hoped for, though.

The sixth cubicle contained what could best be described as a chocolate-coated Pop Tart smothered mayonnaise - and that was *after* the visitor's twice-failed attempt to flush the bastard down.

The last thing anyone needed.

This morning - some fifteen hours post-incident - the offending turd was still living the high life within the bowl.

The consistency of the shit had of course subdued. The red and dark brown and congealed together and formed a sort of repugnant tarred puss.

That was sort of the idea, though. If it could break down, then it'd be easier to shift.

Willy yanked down on the flush and stood back, arms folded, and watch the toilet guzzle down the turd.

The water swirled and bubbled over it as the powerful flush did its thing. Once the foam spread away, the damned fecal matter was still bobbing in the water.

Willy tutted and hit the flush once again. This time, slightly less powerful on account of the cistern not filling up as it should.

And, once again, the foamy bubbles sheathed the magic trick.

But it didn't do the job. The turd bobbed up and down to its own sanctimonious fanfare. You'll never beat me, its body shape threatened.

Willy slammed the lid down in anger and shook his head.

A few moments later, the sixth cubicle was locked. A sign saying *"out of order"* plastered to the door. This was going to be a job for Willy when the place was less busy.

One cubicle down? Big deal. It was early days yet, and Willy had one or two tricks up his sleeve - or, more specifically, in his stock cupboard - that he could play on the insistent shit if push came to shove.

For now, at around 9:30 am, the mall was in full swing. Because the shops were busy this meant that Willy was busy, too.

As he scratched off the ceramic on the basin, a man stood up at the urinal and took his penis.

Of course, Willy didn't see it. He knew what was happening by the man's action. It sounds somewhat facile to say that Willy had guessed what the man was doing. Upwards of around two hundred men would be doing the same thing during the course of the day.

Something didn't seem right with this guy, though. Willy looked up and stop scratching the basin. He peered into the mirror, looking over his own shoulder.

"Yeah, yeah. Here we come," the man shifted his hips and removed *himself* out of his zipper, "Yeah. Oooh."

Willy squinted and moved his head into the mirror. A bit too close. The man relieving himself faced away as he began to empty his bladder.

Then, a long streak of dark, yellow water hit the air freshener cake, "Awww, yes. Yeah, that's good. That's good."

Willy ducked his head and breathed a sigh of relief. The constant stream of urine was a great source of comfort. For a split second, it seemed as if the man might have been doing something else.

The urinating man whistled to himself as he peed into the urinal. A strong stench of musky hops wafted under Willy's nose. He felt like coughing.

And so he did.

It caught the attention of the man in mid-stream. He turned over his shoulder and caught Willy looking at him in the mirror.

"What are you looking at?"

Willy double-took and looked down at the basin.

"Yeah, that's right," the man shook the urine drops from the end of his penis. "You're paid to clean. So, clean."

The man's zipper screeched up to a close. He wiped off his hands on his blazer and made his way to the basin beside Willy.

The man placed his hands under the tap and thumped down the cold water knob, "You usually watch punters when they have a piss, do ya?"

Willy didn't answer. Instead, he busied himself with cleaning the basin in front of him.

"Eh?" he shook the excess water from his hands, "What's the matter? Cat got your tongue? Answer me, *coon*."

Willy didn't rise to the racial slur, nor the threat.

The urinal flushed by itself. In a largely soundless environment, the action caused Willy's spine to tingle. The later rumbling of the pipes behind the wall didn't help calm his nerves.

"Yeah, I thought so," the man chuckled to himself and adjusted his collar in the mirror, "Just a lowlife cleaner, aren't ya?"

Willy nodded, hoping his affirmation might allay any confrontation.

The man reached into the metal holder on the wall and took out a wedge of tissue paper. He dried his hands and kept an eye on Willy

"They pay you much for this job, do they?"

Willy closed his eyes and reached under his left arm. He felt around and coughed.

"Nah, didn't think so," the man scrunched the paper towel and tossed it into the bin. He made his way to the door and opened it. A sound of commotion came through from the corridor.

"Minimum wage monkey. A word of advice, mate. You gotta stop perving on the punters."

The door slammed shut behind him.

Willy stood up straight and turned on the tap. He ran his hands under the water and splashed some to his face.

As he opened his eyes, he saw himself stare back. Yes, he was dark-skinned. Very dark-skinned. Being of African origin, this shouldn't have been much of a surprise. Did that give the man license to call him names? Of course it didn't.

Willy knew that his job wasn't looked at favorably by the public at large. Hell, he didn't even carry any authority around here at all. Willy was at the mercy of many inspections and a boss who didn't much care for him.

A repetitive banging noise came from the other side of the gents door.

"Mister. Mister," a muffled voice pleaded from behind the door handle.

Willy ran over to the door and opened it. He found a teenage boy banging on the office door, "Mister, open up."

Willy clapped his hands together, getting the boy's attention.

"Mister. Come, quick."

The boy ran off around the corner and into the corridor. Willy followed him.

Two teenage boys rocked the coke machine back and forth. A gaggle of terrified shoppers lined the corridor, watching them attack the machine.

The first lad, a chubby ginger kid, punched the window with all his puny might, "The machine won't gimme my drink."

"Smash the glass, man," the second kid growled, clinging against the side of the dangerously heavy machine.

"Hey," Willy screamed. "Get down."

"Nar, mister," the second kid cackled and kicked the side of the machine. "The bloody drinks machine is knackered."

The ginger boy stepped back and ran toward the machine with his fist, "Agggghhh."

He smashed the window apart as his friend barged into the side of it.

Dozens of tins of coke, lemonade, and various bottles of pop flew out of their spirals and slammed onto the ground.

"Hey," screamed a security guard, legging it down the corridor. He barged his way past some of the onlookers.

The vending machine rocked back and forth, threatening to topple over.

"Stop those kids."

Willy stepped back and held out his hands, suggesting his innocence.

"Go on. Knock the bastard over," cackled the chubby ginger kid.

The second boy took a running barge and completed his mission. The machine tipped over and crashed onto its side. The impact narrowly missed the child who'd brought Willy over.

"Whoa, man."

"Okay, you fat little shit," the security guard yelled, "Get away from that."

"Gerroff me," he screamed as the security guard manhandled him away from the machine, "This is assault."

The security guard radioed for assistance, "Twelve-four, this is four-six, over."

"This is twelve-four, what is it?"

"Vandalism on the southern perimeter walkway."

"On our way," came the response.

The second kid held out his hands and offered the security guard a fight, "Don't touch my friend, you pado."

"You," the security guard yelled whilst restraining the chubby ginger kid, "Stay there. Willy, can you get him, please?"

Willy stepped forward and grabbed the second kid by the shoulder, who retaliated instinctively, "Get off me, you black bastard."

The security guard shooed the onlookers away, "Okay, nothing to see here. It's all under control."

By now, both the guard and Willy had a child in each hand, preventing them from running away.

An ocean of dark, sticky cola ran around the soles of their shoes.

"Right, what's your name?" the security guard asked the ginger kid, "Why aren't you at school?"

he ginger kid spat into the security guard's face. His friend found it hilarious, "School's *gay*. And so are you."

Willy kept the second, smaller child in his grip. He observed the spillage from the vending machine.

Several two pounds coins had tumbled from the coin compartment. The stench of cola and red soda pop surrounding their feet was intense.

"Let me go," the second kid yelled. "This is assault, man."

Willy tightened his grip on the boy's shoulder, "Owwww."

He wrenched the kid back and bent the boy's arm around his back, just above his waist.

"*Rape*," screamed the kid. "This pedo's molesting me."

"Shut up," screamed the security guard.

The second kid spat to the floor, wide-eyed with venom, "Yeah? Make me, you nonce."

"Nonce, huh?" the security chuckled, barely able to contain his anger, "Let's see how *gangster* you are when we call your parents, you little turd."

9:45 am. Technically, it wasn't Willy's job to mop up the sea of cola from the corridor. It would be a while for an on-call cleaner to come down and carry out their duty. So, Willy offered to do it.

Not out of the kindness of his heart. He did it so that he could clear the way for shoppers to use his facilities.

Willy erected a cordon reading - *"Caution! Slippery Surface."* Underneath it, a symbol displayed a silhouetted stick-man in mid-slip. Willy snorted to himself as he mopped the sticky stuff away from the middle of the floor.

The liquid he was clearing was anything but slippery. It had an abrasive, unrelenting gluey aspect to it.

It was easy to get lost in your thoughts as you mopped away, he thought. Willy was never one for listening to music on his phone as he worked. All he was left with was his thoughts.

Since when did it all become so hostile and violent, he wondered. When he first took on the role as supervisor of the facilities at Kaleidoscope, the children behaved like children. They were obedient and largely well behaved. Not the monstrous, venom-riddled ADHD critters they have now.

These days, everything was the opposite. No respect. No reverence for authority or their elders.

The fallen vending machine was a testament to that notion. There it was, laying on its side. The flap where you put your hand in to retrieve your goods acted as a mouth, groaning for its life.

The shattered glass pane, rendering the device a shadow of its former self.

And there Willy was, squeezing the liquid out through the grill. It looked like blood, but it smelt of strawberry soda. There was so much of it.

Willy felt sorry for the vending machine. Was he going out of his tiny mind? He used to have a cat many years ago before his wife passed away and his daughter left home. His attitude toward it was anthropomorphic, to say the least.

Lately, Willy had been ascribing the same sentiment to inanimate objects.

Take his mop, for example. Its name was Queenie.

He'd had it for twenty-five years. It was older than his own daughter.

It had several brushes over the years. The metal neck housing needed replacing three times since he bought it. Nevertheless, it was still Queenie.

She'd been with him since the old days. A one constant in his life and career who'd never let him down.

"My big fat Willy," came a voice from behind him, followed by a large hand on his shoulder. He closed his eyes and sighed to himself. The voice was familiar and totally expected.

Willy turned around to see a large black man with sunglasses in front of him. He had a large rucksack over his shoulder.

"You not happy to see a bredren, man?"

Willy half-smiled and shook the man's hand. He nodded over to his office.

The man turned back to Willy and licked his lips, "Yeah, brah."

Willy closed the door as the man took a seat at the desk. His name was Ian - an old friend of Willy's. His manner was caustic, yet strangely affable. His towering height and large frame were threatening.

Just ask the poor plastic seat he was sitting on.

"Never fails to astound me, you know," Ian looked around and scanned the contents of the office.

A laptop and old CRT monitor on a rickety wooden desk. Papers scattered all over it. They looked like invoices and receipts.

On the wall, a large calendar for the year ahead. Most of the entries were unfilled.

A fan in the corner of the room that had collected dust. It clearly hadn't been used in years.

To the right of the desk, a large safe nestled between two filing cabinets.

"Yo, Willy," the man lifted his rucksack and slammed it

onto the table, "Take a seat."

Willy walked around the table, trying not to look at the bag. Ian unzipped it half way and became impatient, "Sit your beautiful, black ass down on the chair."

Willy sat in the chair and placed his hands on the counter.

"That's better," Ian huffed and gripped the zipper on the rucksack. He rolled his shoulders and indicated the fan in the corner of the room.

"Bit hot in here, innit?" Ian asked.

Willy shrugged and looked away.

"Ah, I get it, now," Ian smiled and pulled the zipper down, "The fan's bust, right?"

Willy nodded and looked at the rucksack. Ian took out a large parcel wrapped in cling film. From the way Ian held it, it must have been very heavy.

He dropped it to the table and took out a second parcel. He placed it next to the first.

Before long, Ian had retrieved ten of them. Two piles of five. He slid the rucksack to one side and took out a pocket knife.

"See this here, Willy Bee?"

Willy nodded. He was nervous.

"Man's gonna keep them tight here for me, yeah?" Ian pulled out the blade and poked it into the side of the top parcel. A white powder fell onto the side.

"Pure Colombian, man. Mother nature's pick-me-up," Ian giggled and snorted the powder in one hit. His head flew back and the knife clanged to the table.

"Whoa, man. Brraaaa," Ian wiped his nostril with his knuckle and blinked at the ceiling light, "Shit."

Willy looked at the fallen powder on the table and wondered if he should reach for it.

It was beautiful and inviting.

"Nah," Ian thumped the desk, causing some of the remnants to dance around the table top, "You don't touch this *'ting*, you hear? You keep it here like usual. Till I come back for it. Okay?"

Willy nodded, afraid for his life. He coughed violently into his fist.

"The hell, man?" Ian said, wiping his lips. "You sniffed a piece just there?"

Willy shook his head.

"You gotta cold or sumthin'?"

Willy sniffed and shook his head.

"Open the safe, brah."

Following Ian's instruction, Willy slid off his chair and spun the dial around on the safe lock. Left, then right. Finally, it sprang open.

"Okay, man. Lift them in."

Ian passed two parcels over to Willy. He reached deep inside the safe and planted them in.

Then, the next two.

It wasn't too long before all ten parcels were parked right at the back of the dwelling.

Ian stood up and threw the rucksack into Willy's arms. He caught it but didn't know what to do next.

"Put it at the front, innit?" Ian suggested. "Block the view if anyone gets in."

Willy did as instructed. He fanned out the emptiness of the material and threw the straps back. If anyone got into the safe without Willy's knowledge, they'd be greeted with an innocuous bag.

"Lock the 'ting, man."

Willy turned the lock's dial around and yanked on the handle. Fully locked.

Ian looked at his wristwatch.

"It's tenna clock, now. I gotta meetin' with Damien at four, so you gonna hold it for me till then, okay?"

Willy rose to his feet and nodded.

"You're a good boy, Willy. Doin' this for me, ya nah," Ian smiled and grabbed him by his shoulder, "But, see if I get here at four and my shit's gone…"

Willy started to quake in his boots. Ian meant business.

Convenience

"… I'mma kill you."

Chapter 2
10:00 – 11:00

Ian made his way out of the office leaving Willy a little worse for wear. The two men had known each other for years. Ian would often visit with things for Willy to "hold on to" while he went about his business.

As Willy span the dial around on the safe, he felt the light clicks within the device rumble through his fingers. Each click, click, click felt like a punch to the face.

A quick glance at the wall clock revealed that the morning was in full swing. Even though the office door was quite thick, the hustle and bustle of the business day crept through it.

A stampede of people seemed to be flowing toward the public toilets. The faint, bleached-out silhouettes from the punters moved left and right past frosted glass pane on the door.

Willy felt a beeping noise come from his trouser leg. The surface of his mobile phone's screen lit up through the fabric. He reached in and pulled out it.

Sorry, Willy. Am sick. Can't come in 2day. Apologies, Sheila.

Willy sighed. He knew what this meant. Today was late night shopping at the Kaleidoscope. This meant an hour's extra opening time for his facilities. The stores closed at eight but, in the management's infinite wisdom, all the public conveniences closed two hours earlier. The only facilities available after that time were in the restaurants.

Willy walked out of the office carrying something in his arms. His trainers stepped one in front of another as a flurry of pink shoes and high heels raced around them.

Then, the legs of the stand hit the shiny surface in front of the ladies toilet. Willy stepped back and looked at the sign. It advised that a male attendant would be attending to the ladies facility today. Patrons shouldn't be alarmed. Of course, if anyone should want to contest this fact they were more than welcome to visit the office for an explanation.

Willy hoped it wouldn't have to come to that. He looked at his clipboard and grabbed the pen. On the hour, every hour, both facilities needed to be checked that they hadn't become dirty and unusable.

A rubbish jazz version of *Think Twice* by Celine Dion piped through the walls, underscoring Willy's disappointment. He took a deep breath and pushed his way into the ladies toilet.

The first two cubicles had their doors shut. Presumably locked. The remaining four seemed clean enough as Willy scanned them. The washbasins looked untouched. A quick blast of water in the third basin would clear out the straggly bits of black hair. It wasn't worth scooping them out of the bowl and putting into the bin.

The fact that the first two cubicles were occupied spooked Willy.

A shuffling came from the first cubicle, followed by a clanking sound. Like the heels of a pair of shoes thudding against the floor.

"Oh, oh. *Shit*," a woman's voice hushed from within the cubicle, "This bloody thing, man. I swear to God."

The woman was clearly in distress.

"What's wrong, babe?" came a higher-tone female voice from the second cubicle.

"My tampon's got stuck."

Willy blinked and put one foot in front of the other, careful to avoid drawing attention to himself. He made his way to the cubicles and saw the woman's red high heel shoes kicking around on the ground.

From the angle he had, he could see that the woman had raised her left leg up and placed her shoe on the rim of the seat. One foot precariously danced around the floor.

"Aww, *man*," screamed the lady in the first cubicle.

"Want me to come in there and help you, love?"

"Naw. It's just this thing's *so* fiddly."

As Willy kept an eye on her girl's red shoe, a sloppy, blood-infused tampon slapped to the floor. Specks of red liquid coughed around the ceramic, contrasting with the pristine white tiled floor.

"Oh, bollocks," the woman huffed. "I dropped the bastard."

"Well pick it up, then."

"Duh. I will."

Willy kept his head hung low as he saw the woman's long, blond hair fall under the door. She lowered her head and bent over to pick up the detritus-ridden length of blood-soaked cotton.

"Got it."

Willy closed his eyes as the fingers crept around the messy tampon.

The sound of the tampon hitting the toilet bowl followed shortly after that.

"Right, that's that done."

Willy arched his back and stood up straight.

"Hey, you seen that guy who works here? The cleaner bloke?"

"Yeah," the tampon lady's voice whirled over the gap above the door, "What about him?"

"He's weird, isn't he?"

"Can't say I've really noticed," the lady cleared her throat and shuffled her hips, "Right, that's the bastard in. I got it. Thank God for that."

"You all good, love?"

"Yeah. Got a few spots of claret on my knickers, but, *whatever*."

Both her feet hit the floor. A pair of hands reached down and grabbed the bridged knickers between her ankles. It yanked them up the calves of the woman.

The toilet flushed a few seconds later.

Willy immediately felt the urge to leave the ladies toilet. Any moment now, the two girls would emerge and catch him there.

But this was his workplace. He was entitled to be inside the ladies toilet when he was on duty. The sign advertising his presence was all he needed.

Looking down the length of his shirt and trousers, clipboard in hand, it didn't much look like he was working. No, if they were to emerge now, he'd look a bit of a pervert.

In that split second, Willy felt out of place. Should anyone walk in now, they might not have taken him for an employee.

The second cubicle's toilet flushed.

"Right, let's get out of here. There's a dress in *Then* I've got my eye on."

Willy widened his eyes and made for the door. An overweight woman pushed it open and nearly walked into him.

"Oh my. I'm sorry—" she tried as Willy barged past her, "Hey."

Willy turned the corner and pushed the door to his office open. He slipped through, yanked the door shut and closed his eyes, catching his breath.

Three loud thuds on the frosted glass plane immediately followed. The noise snapped Willy out of his slight stupor.

"Hey. Excuse me."

Willy leaned into the glass and tried to figure out who

the woman might be.

"I know you're in there. Can you open up please?"

Willy rubbed his hand on his shirt and threw the clipboard onto his desk. He took the door handle in his palm and pulled the door open.

He raised his eyebrows at the angry, overweight lady.

"Oi, are you the owner of these toilets?" she asked.

Willy nodded his head.

"Some bloke was hanging out in the girls' toilets just now and ran out when I spotted him."

Willy looked down at the floor and back up at the lady. He wasn't checking her out but she didn't see it that way.

"What are you looking at?"

Glancing over the lady's shoulder, Willy spotted the drinks dispenser repairman making his way down the walkway. He reached knocked-over bending machine and examined the mess.

"Are you listening to me?" screamed the lady. "Some pervert was just in the girls' toilet."

Willy looked back at the lady with a solemn face.

The overweight lady's double chin drooped as the look of realization fell across her face.

"Oh my God," she scanned Willy and pursed her lips. "It was *you*, wasn't it?"

Willy half-smiled and shrugged his shoulders apologetically.

"Oh, how embarrassing," she swallowed back her own embarrassed smirk. The two girls from the cubicles rushed past her, chatting to each other. The blond woman had a strange walk as they entered the walkway that took them to the shops.

Willy pointed at the sign in front of the ladies toilet door. It gently advertised the fact that a male employee would be attending to it.

"Oh, gosh," she grinned. "I'm sorry, I didn't know. I was going to have you reported for a moment, just there."

Willy smiled as politely as he could. He nodded at the

corner of the facility waiting area. A CCTV camera hung in the corner, oscillating every five seconds from left to right.

"Right. You had it all on camera, anyway."

Willy nodded.

The overweight lady stepped back and made her excuses. She headed straight for the ladies toilet, "Sorry, again."

She disappeared through the door in embarrassment. Willy turned to the young man shifting the vending machine back onto its legs.

The man brushed a few fragments of shattered glass along the floor with his left foot, "What a mess. These scummy kids."

He returned to his cart and wheeled it over to the machine. He reached into his pocket and took out his phone.

"Yeah, it's me. They battered it beyond recognition. We're gonna need a new front panel, and a restock. Yeah, I can do that, I have most of the inventory with me."

Satisfied that the man had it all under control, Willy moved back into his office and closed the door.

The public toilets in the southern perimeter had only been open for an hour and twenty minutes. For Willy, it already felt like a lifetime.

The harsh strip lighting in the office wasn't doing his constitution much good. He lost his balance for a brief moment and almost crashed onto the desk.

A remedy was required.

He flung himself onto his chair, causing the casters to roll back and hit the cupboard behind him. He grabbed the safe for balance and pushed himself toward the desk.

From out of his pocket came a small, rectangular tin. He placed it on the table and popped open the lid.

A packet of Rizla papers.

A small pouch of tobacco.

And a tiny baggie stuffed with dark green leaves.

Out came a paper. In went a line of tobacco. Holding the joint between his thumb and forefinger, Willy licked the glued edge with his tongue. He'd done it a million times before now.

A sprinkle of ground leaves lined the brown tobacco.

His tongue slid along the edge. A quick tear from the Rizla cardboard, folded in four and poked into the end completed his elevenses.

He sniffed along the length of the joint and savored the rich aroma. He placed the roach end between his lips and took out a lighter.

The flame came to life and threatened to kiss the paper.

Then, the office door flew open.

"Ah, Willy. You're here."

Willy turned around and scraped the cigarette paraphernalia off the desk. It hit the floor, causing quite the commotion.

The tiny bag of marijuana leaves still sat on the desktop.

"Mind if I have a quick word, Willy?"

Willy shook his head, not having noticed the baggie. He was too preoccupied with making eye contact with his boss.

Ted, the *Kaleidoscope*'s operational manager, had a bit of a reputation as a stern and officious nerd. Standing at an unfathomable 6'7", his figure was imposing. Less imposing were his glasses and overall effete manner.

Still, the guy meant business. He'd recently laid off several of the shopping mall's employees. Willy was always anxious around Ted. The shopping mall expanded during a recent staff restructure. It accommodated twenty new units in its annexe at the north end of the complex.

One entire removal of a set of facilities near the cinema suffered as a result. This redevelopment necessitated a streamlining of three permanent cleaners. Ted referred to them as waste disposal operatives.

Overnight, in the space of a few hours, five operatives were let go.

Willy coughed into his sleeve and acted as normal as he possibly could.

Ted took his seat, adjusted his glasses and laid a set of papers out in front of him, "You look like hell, Willy. Everything okay?"

Willy nodded and coughed into his sleeve once again.

"Okay, if you insist," Ted clasped his hands together, "Look, Willy, I just wanted to give you a heads-up."

Willy raised his eyebrows. He'd heard the rumors of furthering restructuring. This was an official follow-up. Today of all days.

"Yeah, it's just that I've had it come from head office. There is going to be a restructure next month."

Ted pointed to a detailed proposal on the sheet of paper in front of him, "The entire south-facing facade is being renovated. You knew that right?"

Willy nodded and wiped his sleeve across his lip.

"Yes, this has been in the works for a while. They're redoing the entire network of roads and pulling the one-way system. No news there, but take a look at this."

Ted traced his fingers to the sketch of the southern block, "They're going to be shifting all the perimeter shops north to increase footfall. In effect, the entire southern walkway is to be remodeled. It'll extend to the car park."

Ted looked up at Willy for a response. He thought he'd find some protest from his employee. Instead, Ted found a strong sense of apathy.

"Do you understand what I'm saying, Willy?"

Willy nodded and folded his arms. He didn't want to put up a fight. He wanted Ted gone. Willy couldn't care less about the redesign and impending redundancy - if that's what Ted was aiming for.

"The entire southern walkway. The coffee shop. The information booth. These facilities. They're all being removed in their entirety or shifted elsewhere."

Willy shrugged his shoulders. There was nothing he could do about any of this news.

"You don't talk much, do you?"

Willy shook his head and looked at his hands atop the table. Then, he spotted the baggy of marijuana a few inches to the left.

Ted hadn't spotted it.

"There have been reports from various staff members, Sheila included, that you're unwell, Willy. I can't say it hasn't gone unnoticed by me, either."

Willy closed his eyes for two seconds and opened them again.

"Okay, you've nothing to say. That's fine," Ted stood to his feet, collected his papers and made for the door, "The board are meeting tomorrow afternoon to finalize the proposals. We should have something concrete for you and Sheila early next week."

Willy stood up and smiled. He nodded his head in approval.

"Oh," Ted opened the door and nodded at the tiny baggy on the table, "You take care today, yeah?"

Willy looked at the baggy and back at Ted. He received a knowing wink from his boss as he exited the office.

The office went quiet. Usually, the ticking of the wall clock went unnoticed by Willy. Right now, though, it sounded like seven hundred decibels.

TICK, TICK, TICK…

Christ, that sound was annoying. Queenie stared back at her owner from the corner of the room.

Willy made eyes at the safe. For the first time in the twelve years since management installed the beast, the dial looked like a nose.

The handle underneath resembles a slanted, blackened mouth. Was it smiling at him, or frowning? The two metal hinges could have been the eyes if they were sloped.

Willy grabbed Queenie by the neck and made his way

out of the office.

Determined to perform the hour's clean-up of the ladies facilities, he made a right out of the office. He clocked a woman with her child sitting on the bench opposite the vending machine. The drinks machine repairman was in mid-chatter with the woman who cradled her child in her arms.

Willy made for the door and pushed it open.

The ladies toilet was empty. All cubicle doors sunk inward, indicating that there was no-one inside them. If there were, they'd at least be in a state of decency that afforded him the time to do his job.

Sections of the floor with filthy. Queenie's bristled head hit the surface and pushed forward, collecting up a few scraps of tissue paper and strands of hair.

The pungent objects collected up and moved under the hand dryers.

A quick check of the cubicles was all that had to happen.

The sixth cubicle, farthest away from the door, was the first that Willy inspected. The door flung inward, allowing Willy to look around inside.

The paper towel holder was fine. The seat and the contents of the bowl were clean.

Down came the lid. A reset of the flush handle.

The same for the fifth, fourth, third and second cubicle. Now, all immaculate.

Then, the first cubicle. Willy took a deep breath and pushed the door in with his fingers.

He noticed the muzak playing around him as the door to the first cubicle moved in.

Willy stepped in and gasped.

Six bloodied tampons hung from the cubicle wall. They'd been taped by the stringy ends to the wall.

The walls seemed to vibrate as a flood of water shot through the pipes. The rumbling was unsettling.

Above the cistern, a message written in bloody effluence stared back at Willy.

I KNOW WHAT YOU DID.

The letters "K and "Y" had slopped down the tiles, creating quite the disgusting mess. It was written on purpose. Designed for Willy's attention.

He pinched his nose shut between his fingers and threw Queenie toward the basins.

Willy yelped and stepped back, pulling the door shut. He buried his thumbnail into the horizontal slit on the outer side of the lock and bolted it shut.

His chest sucked in as he took the imagery into his moment for the briefest of moments. Who could have done this? When could they have done it?

Queenie couldn't clear this up, and no-one could afford to enter the first cubicle.

Time was of the essence.

Willy opened the stockroom door and grabbed a jiffy cloth, a plastic bag and a bottle of disinfectant. He shut the door and made his way back to the ladies toilet.

Once inside, he stepped toward the first cubicle. The pipes groaned around him as his trainers squeaked across the freshly-cleaned flooring.

He held out his hand and slid his thumbnail into the lock's slit. Turning it around, he knew the door would fling forward the moment it unbolted.

As the door swung in, a woman entered the ladies toilet.

The door pushed open as Willy turned around to see the woman stop in her tracks.

She gasped, not expecting a sullen, thin black man to be in there.

"You scared me," the woman exclaimed. "You're in the wrong—"

"—Shhhh," Willy held his index finger to his lips and nodded at the first cubicle.

He waved her out of the toilet, but she wouldn't oblige him. She simply stared at him, wondering what the hell was going on.

Willy turned to the first cubicle and stepped inside.

There were no tampons hanging from the wall. No message scrawled in blood on the tiles.

By all accounts, the cubicle was spotless.

Willy couldn't believe his eyes. The cleaning apparatus slipped from his palm and hit the floor.

The impact of the items crashing around his feet startled the woman.

She moved toward the cubicles as a light sobbing emitted from the first of them.

"Hello?" She carefully placing one foot in front of the other, "Are you okay in there?"

As she kept moving forward, the sobbing grew stronger.

"Shall I call someone? Get you some help?"

No reply. Just more sobbing. The stress of the day was getting to Willy.

She peered around the corner and pushed the door forward. She found Willy on his knees, doubled-over on the floor and crying his eyes out.

"Oh, my," she crouched down behind him, "Umm, are you okay?"

It was an awkward situation to be in. The woman only came to the toilet to relieve herself. She hadn't accounted for trying to console a janitor in the middle of his own place of work.

The woman looked up and around the cubicle. She was puzzled. Why would a gentleman be in there shedding tears all over the floor?

She clocked the cleaning paraphernalia and put two and two together. The man worked here.

The woman rubbed his back and tried to console him,

"Shall I call someone for you?"

Willy sniffed and shook his head.

"It's okay," she took his back into her arms and knelt him upright, "It's okay."

Willy sniffed once again and choked back his tears. He kept looking down at his knees. Life was conspiring to keep him down.

The woman cradling him in her arms, "Take your time, sweetie."

***

10:35 am. Willy sat on one of five stone benches at the outer entrance of the Kaleidoscope. The gushing fountain opposite him emitted a semi-laugh. He stared blankly at the cars that whizzed past and then at the top of the fountain. A five-pronged star made of stone nestled atop the spraying water. It looked like a crown, standing proud, twenty-feet high atop the structure.

Before the summer holidays, hearsay floated among the locals. It was alleged that the Kaleidoscope Shopping Mall had been a target for a group of radicalized terrorists. The plan was thwarted by the secret service, or some such outfit. Willy would have been at work that day if they had attacked.

Something about a car full of TATP explosives.

No-one knew if the rumor was true, though. The nearby school was attacked by two teenagers that morning. It shook the community to the core. The citizens of Chrome Valley were very alert as a result. In the intervening months since that event, the mood had softened.

Willy secretly wished that the gossip was true, after all. If those terrorists had been successful, the car would have smashed through the fountain and plowed through the department store.

If the car had been packed with explosives, the entire

southern perimeter would have been obliterated. It would have killed anyone in a one-hundred-foot radius at least, including those in the convenience.

Willy wasn't at work that day, though.

Instead, he was at the hospital getting results from a blood test.

Just his luck, really.

Not even the sight of the children splashing around in the fountain cheered him up. As he rolled his joint between his fingers on his lap, he focused on a seven-year-old girl with blonde hair. She scooped up some water from the fountain moat and threw it over the head of a little boy.

He giggled through his soaking wet shirt and gave as good as he took. He drenched the poor girl. Instead of chuckling back, she screamed. Her squeals alerted her mother who was sitting on the opposite bench.

"Oi. You little brat," the mother tore herself away from her phone call, "Get away from that fountain."

"But *mom*."

"I said now," she snapped and returned to her call. She shifted the bags of shopping away from her feet and raced over to her daughter.

"Get out of the water, Lilly," she said and yanked her daughter back to the benches by her soaking wet shirt. The girl's feet kicked out as she screamed along the waterlogged path.

Willy threw the joint in his lips and tucked his right hand under his left arm. Deep into the pit, he prodded around and sighed.

He retrieved his plastic lighter and shifted along the bench, away from an elderly woman. She stared up at the mall's entrance, awe-struck by its size. A shiny gold earring hung above her left shoulder. It was difficult not to spot.

Willy tore his eyes away from her gold earring and took the opportunity to gaze skyward along with the lady. Yes, the Kaleidoscope Shopping Mall was a grand affair, to be sure.

He flicked the lighter and sparked up the end of his joint. A plume of smoke shot down past his esophagus and down his neck, blanketing both lungs.

Willy held in the smoke and smiled at the mother as she berated her daughter. A swift smack to the buttocks seemed to curtail any nonsense from the brat.

He shook his head and blew out the smoke down his sleeve in an attempt to not draw attention to himself.

Willy closed his eyes and bent his head left and right, ironing out the kinks in his neck.

The smoke felt good. He was immediately relaxed. Every muscle in his body seemed to slow down and stop working.

The lighter slipped between his fingers and hit the ground.

As he bent down to pick it up, water-soaked boy beat him to it. He grabbed it in his hands and offered Willy his lighter, "This yours, mister?"

Willy nodded and held out his hand. The boy pulled his hand away and chuckled, "Nar. You gotta give me somethin'."

Willy shrugged his shoulders. What could he give the boy? A puff from his joint? No, he didn't think that would be appropriate.

"You got any money on ya?" the kid asked.

"Oi. Daryl.." his mother screamed from the opposite bench, "Give the man his lighter back."

The kid wiped the water from his brow and shot Willy a stern look, "You can have it for a fiver."

Willy snorted and snatched the lighter out of the kid's hand with an expediency usually demonstrated by magicians - or pickpockets.

"Hey," the boy protested.

"Daryl," his mother screamed at the top of her lungs, " I said leave the man alone and get your ass over here, you little shit."

The kid huffed at his mother and turned to Willy, "Prick."

He made his way over to his mother and got the same punishment his sister had received not two minutes earlier. A good clip around the ear.

Willy roared with laughter and took a long, deep toke on his joint.

The mother and her two children moved away from the bench. Each of them in a state of fury.

But who cared? Willy didn't. He chugged the lightning-fast joint down to its nub.

"It's so big, isn't it?" the elderly lady muttered to herself. She said it loud enough in the hope that anyone nearby might contribute to the conversation.

Willy looked back at the facade. It loomed over both of them, and all the incoming shoppers. A giant clock hung in the center of the frontage, like one, huge Big Brother-esque eye.

The elderly woman turned to Willy and spotted him sucking down the contents of his joint. To avoid making eye contact, he looked down and noticed her ridiculous bright red shoes. Two yellow sunflower broaches sat atop the toes on each foot.

"Those things will kill you, you know," she chuckled.

Willy snorted and coughed out a lungful of smoke. It was the funniest remark he'd heard all morning.

A final toke and flick of the roach shot the joint into the fountain, never to be seen again.

Willy shuffled back into the Kaleidoscope in a haze of merriment and general uplift. A tinny muzak version of Katrina and the Waves' *Walking on Sunshine* rumbled around the speakers. To Willy, it felt like it was playing at an unusually high volume. He was somewhat giddy after his cheeky little smoke, after all.

The shoppers seemed to move hyper-fast, yet in ultra-slow-motion. Were they going so quick that the shapes of their bodies were blurring? Or were they moving so slowly that their souls outpaced their physical form?

To Willy, it didn't matter much. The information desk loomed as he walked his merry way to the southern perimeter.

The attractive blond assistant seemed to wave back at him. "Hey, Willy."

He waved back, grinning from ear to ear. He moved past the information desk and gave her a wink. She returned the sentiment.

He clapped his hands together and danced his way in tune to the outrageously crap version of the song. Willy couldn't have looked any less cool than this. It was the funniest thing the assistant - and her punters - had seen all morning.

A couple of children joined in the dance with Willy. They stepped forward, clapped their hands, and shook their heads - all at the right time. It was a momentary wave of joy in an otherwise full and drab day.

Two loud, electronic beeps fired around the walkway. Each one acted like a punch in the face for Willy.

Smack. His head flung backward. The second beep throttled him across the face, sending his lips shimmering toward the coffee store.

Willy gasped and opened his eyes. He'd fallen asleep at his desk in his office. The quick shunting of his hands moved the half-smoked marijuana joint across the desk.

He blew the black ash from the desktop in haste. His hand slid across to the side, collecting up the burnt ends.

He blinked a couple of times and tried to acclimatise himself to his surroundings

"Yo. Willy," came a low gruff voice from over his shoulder.

Willy closed his eyes. There was no-one in the room with him. If he kept them shut long enough, perhaps he could be convinced that he was hearing things.

"Willy. You dumb coon," the voice threatened, "Turn around and look at me."

Willy turned his head over his shoulder as slowly as he could. All he could see were two fragile cupboards and the safe nestled between them.

He blinked a couple of times and breathed a sigh of relief. The handle of the safe shunted downward and split into two thin strips.

"Remember what I told you, Willy," the safe barked as the dial above its handle sniffed and scrunched itself.

Willy nodded rapidly and held out his hands.

"If they get inside me, you're gonna die, right?"

Willy didn't know how to respond. He held his fist against his chest and patted the safe *on the head* to assure it that he would play ball.

"Good boy, Willy," the safe's dial-nose spun around revealing the unlock code: 1, 1, 8. "Although, we all know the code, don't we?"

Willy dived off his chair and hit the floor knees-first in front of the safe and grabbed at the dial. Frantic, he spun it around, hoping to scramble the number once again.

The safe handle's lips moved as the hulking device laughed at him, "Night, night. Willy Gee."

The handle swung down and locked. Willy spun the dial to three random numbers and caught his breath.

He ducked his head, his chin resting on his chest. The cacophony of shoppers milling around was the only thing he could hear from the other side of the door.

A few people moved past the window, on their way to and from the toilets.

Willy took a few deep breaths. Only this time, his lungs seemed to pulse. The feeling of a hot poker spearing through both organs. It hurt to breathe.

His phone beeped twice from within his trouser pocket. He took the device out and swiped the screen up.

A text message from someone named Maxine.

Convenience

R we still meeting at 12? Love, M xxx

A smile streaked across his face as he read the message. He typed his response.

Yes, of course. C u then. Love, Dad x

Willy walked out of the office and locked the door behind him. He made his way to the gents.

The effect of the joint still rattled around in his head. It caused him to find even the banalest things somewhat amusing. His stomach began to turn.

He started to feel sick.

The sensation of liquid swung around his insides as he moved into the gents toilet. The liquid bounding around inside his stomach threatened to explode like a viciously-shaken bottle of soda.

The cubicles were a mere ten footsteps away. To Willy, it seemed like miles.

He clutched his stomach and ran over to the urinals. The fifth one along seemed the most inviting - and the most clean. The last of the flush cleared the ceramic away for him.

Willy launched himself forward and skidded on his knees. He grabbed the sides of the urinal in both hands and hung his head into the bowl.

A blast of thick vomit flew out from his throat. It splashed against the *WhiffGone* soap cake resting on the grill, pushing it up the curve of the ceramic.

The first jet of vomit was bad enough. Globs of it shot back up into his face, as he yawned his mouth open for a second round of puke

Another good emptying of his stomach slammed into the urinal, splashing most of it back into his face.

"Uggghhh," Willy groaned and spit a few times into the urinal. His tongue hung out of his mouth, keeping the thin ropes of saliva taut between his lips and the cake of soap.

It felt like he had expunged most of the contents of his stomach. But he knew there was at least one more round to go.

Sure enough, it came. The last of whatever undigested food in him jet-streamed into the urinal. He clenched the sides of it so hard, it nearly came off in his hands.

Puke shot out of his nostrils.

He pressed his finger to his right nostrils and fired out a chunk of spew from his left, "Ugh."

"Mister, are you okay?" came a young voice to his right.

Willy squeezed his eyes shut and turned to his right. He was greeted by a tiny penis resting over a tiny forefinger at the sixth and smallest urinal. The end of it opened up, releasing a stream of pee into the ceramic.

Was a little, urinating penis talking to him?

"Have you just been sick?" the penis said, or so it seemed.

Willy blinked and looked up at the body of the person who'd asked the question.

A small frame...

A set of shoulders...

A soft neck...

... and a cute face. A six-year-old boy stood at the urinal waiting to relieve himself, "Ugh, you've been sick."

The boy continued to pee as Willy's face, inches to the left, looked up at him.

"That's disgusting. The cleaner will be really angry at you," the boy offered as he finished peeing. He shook his little dick around, sprinkling droplets of urine in all directions.

The flush at his urinal fired up and drank down the yellow mixture.

Willy gripped the urinal and spat onto the cake, gasping for air.

"Billy," a man yelled from the gent's door, "I told you two minutes, maximum."

Willy looked to his left to see a large man looking at

him. A compromising position for Willy to have been in. On his knees between the child's legs, gasping for life.

"Daddy," the kid yelled as he zipped his pants up, "This black man's just been sick."

"What," the man stormed through the gents toilet and grabbed the boy by his arm. He pushed him back and turned to Willy as he scrambled to his feet.

"What's going on here? What were you doing with my son?" asked the man, inches away from an outright physical assault.

Willy held out his hands and shook his hand.

"He didn't do anything, Daddy," the boy interjected. "He was being sick."

"He wasn't *being* sick," the father screamed. "He *is* sick! Look at him, on his knees, trying to touch you."

"No, Daddy, he wasn't trying—"

The father grabbed Willy by his shirt collar and pulled him forward, face-to-face, "I know what you *men* get up to in here. You're sick."

"Daddy. No—"

"—Shut up," his father turned from his son and back to Willy. The tips of their noses almost scraped together, "Did you touch my kid?"

Willy shook his head in defiance.

"He never did anything—"

"—I said shut the hell up," the father let go of Willy's collar and grabbed his son by the arm, "Right, let's get out of here. Goddamn pedophile *scum* everywhere."

As the father and son reached the door, the man turned back to Willy. A couple of other punters hung around the open door, waiting for the commotion to die down.

The man yanked Billy's arms and pushed him through the door, "I'm going to report you."

"But, Dad—"

"—No, son. We're going to make a formal complaint."

Willy didn't know what to do. He pulled down the creases in his shirt.

The two punters looked at him from the doorway. They wondered if they shouldn't just hold whatever it was they needed to do in for a while longer.

"Man, are you okay?" one of them asked.

Willy nodded and walked over to the adjacent washbasin. He ran the tap and hung his lips sideways across the jet of water.

The two punters made their way to the urinal and unzipped themselves.

"Ugh, what is this?" moaned one of them as he hung his dick over the fifth urinal, "Is that *puke*?"

Willy paused and chose to ignore them. He looked at himself in the mirror and swished the water around in his mouth.

Then, he spat out the contents into the bowl and fanned the stream of water around the tiny fragments of puke. They vanished down the plug hole.

Willy made for the door, keeping a side-eye on the man at the fifth urinal.

He wasn't complaining any longer. Instead, he attempted to spray the rest of the puke down the grill with a stream of piss.

Willy pushed the door open and made his way back to the office.

Chapter 3
11:00 – 12:00

A somewhat disheveled Willy made his way back to the office. He felt his shirt stick to his chest. Some spew marks had splashed against the material when he was sick. He scrunched the material between his fingers and breathed in.

The aroma of spew wafted up his nostrils and crawled into his frontal lobe.

The momentary pause to inhale the stain on his shirt was halted. A woman pushing a buggy flew up the southern perimeter walkway, headed for the main concourse and the shops.

It wasn't her fine figure that caught his attention. Nor was it her outrageously stupid white hat that tilted left and right as she sauntered in the opposite direction. It was the buggy itself. It seemed to have a tiny arm hanging from the side of it.

Willy squinted and tilted his head sideways. The walkway angled over as the arm grew out, attached to a little girl sitting inside it. She moved herself to the side and glanced back at Willy from what felt like miles away.

A row of teeth bleached out through her lips as she smiled at him. The tiny figure disappeared into the distance.

Willy shook his head and felt under his left armpit. His finger prodded around and, for the briefest of moments, his pain subdued. It felt good.

Back in his office, the first thing that caught Willy's attention was the half-smoked joint. It had managed to fall to the floor. He bent over, collected it up and brushed away the burnt ends. A quick blow across the top sent the slivers of burnt paper away.

He held it to his nose and took a deep breath. His eyelids shut to absorb the flavor running deep into his brain.

His eyelids reopened. The wall clock focused into view: 11: 10 am.

Tick, tick, tick.

Willy felt his heart race in time to the faint minute hand making its way past the number two. He smirked to himself, admiring the irony.

Two.

Speaking of which, it was time to clean up the spillage in the gents toilets.

Queenie fell into his palm as if on cue, "Take me," she seemed to say. His trusted old steed had never let him down. If the *Kaleidoscope*'s public convenience was the Roman Colosseum then Queenie was his trusty sword.

Willy took solitude in the fact that he was, at least, surrounded by articles and instruments of the trade. He could rely on them at all times. It was a small and pithy contrivance, to be sure.

It gave him in a sense of belonging. To others, this may have seemed trite and romantic. To Willy, it meant everything - because he had nothing. Certainly nothing *else*, anyway.

A couple of toilet rolls would also come in handy to replenish the dispensers. The first two cubicles were in dire need of restocking. He yanked open the plastic on a package of twelve of them, resting precariously on the cupboard to the left of the safe.

In the true spirit of anthropomorphism, the retrieved

the two rolls as quietly as he could. He didn't want to alert the safe. Not after the stern reminder that it gave him half an hour ago.

Clutching the two rolls in his hand, he pushed the door open and turned left.

Willy approached the gents toilet door. He hadn't expected it to swing out and almost smash him across the face.

It was always a gamble for those who entered. The frosted pane of glass on the door didn't give much of an indication that someone might be headed through it from the other side.

It was pure guesswork. You'd have thought that after twenty or so years of working here that he'd be used to it. Not so much.

The man on the other side seemed to force the door open with an unusual grudge. The door missed Willy's nose as it zipped past his face.

"Oh, I'm sorry," the man apologized and slipped through the door, "Didn't see you there."

Willy smiled shrugged off the incident, still reeling inside. As soon as the man made his merry, recently-relieved way out of the area, Willy ducked his head and held his chest. He felt his heart beat quicker. An attempt was made to swallow down the anxiety. It eventually worked.

And then, the door shut behind him, startling him once again. The toilet roll slipped through his fingers and bounced onto the floor, rolling away from him.

Shit, shit.

The paper roll ran away across the floor, headed for the cubicle area. It left a white, perforated tiling of sheets behind it - like a ball of string used by children in a particularly difficult maze.

Willy bent down and twined the sheets around his hand. Bent over, he made his way along the path the roll had created. The padded toilet tissue that formed the skin of the cardboard interior slimmed down as it paper ran out. It hit the central grille on the tiled floor. The roll changed trajectory and sped straight for the sixth, locked cubicle.

Willy paced along, winding the length of tissue around his hand. It looked like a shitty, makeshift boxing glove by the time he'd reached the cubicles.

Panting and moaning came from behind the second cubicle door as he ran past it, collecting up the tissue.

Dang it if the roll didn't end up rolling under the slit of the sixth cubicle door. Willy huffed and rose to his feet, keeping an eye out for the groaning coming from the second door.

Were the pipes playing up again? The squelching noise that followed suggested that there may be something wrong with the flush or the cistern. Conversely, the noise could have been the occupier trying to pinch off an especially stubborn brown loaf.

Whatever it was, the noise could wait.

Willy slid his protruding thumbnail into the slit of the sixth cubicle's door lock. It turned counter-clockwise.

The door flung in, revealing the three-quarter spent bog roll resting at the bottom of the toilet.

He bent over and picked it up. The roll had seen better days. It had traversed through the clean gents toilet floor. During its journey, it had become a partially soggy collection of hair, footprints, water and yellow spots. There was no way Willy could use it. He couldn't pass this off as a fresh roll and insert it into the holder and hope no-one wouldn't complain.

What if someone had just taken a dump and threw their hand in and tore off a piece? They'd see the detritus-covered ply tissue and discard it, only to discover that the rest were worse.

No, this one was a write-off.

Willy tore off the perforation and set the cardboard

tube onto the dispenser. He looked at his hand. It looked less like a boxing glove and more like a bandage, there was so much of it wrapped around his fist.

The sight of the bandage blurred in Willy's eyes as they focused on the toilet itself. Without a lid, the contents of it stared back at him.

That fifteen-inch turd that refused to go down an hour or so ago was still there. Willy tutted to himself. He tried to block out the groaning noise coming from the second cubicle.

Maybe a hit on the flush would do the trick. He grabbed the handle with his left hand and watched the violent waterfall pummel the shit and try to swallow it down.

It was no use. The turd just bobbed up and down, seemingly laughing right back at Willy's stupid face. It wasn't going anywhere.

What's more, it seemed to have grown in size. Earlier this morning it was around fifteen inches. Now, somewhere near the thirty-inch mark. It had grown so long, it needed to coil itself around the surface of the water and shape of the lower part of the bowl.

"Ah yeah. Ah yeah," someone panted from a few cubicles down. Whoever it was was enjoying their bowel movement a bit *too* much.

The squelching noise was repetitive along with the incessant whining. Willy stepped out of the sixth cubicle and moved past the fifth, fourth and third… and arrived outside the locked second.

He noticed that the first cubicle was also bolted shut.

It wasn't customary, nor professional, for the janitor to bother anyone. Certainly not while there were in situ. It was both company and mall policy to only "infiltrate" a cubicle if there was a cause for concern.

Some elimination of concerns would need to occur about now. The last thing Willy needed was to be reprimanded unduly.

Last year, he barged his way into the third cubicle, thinking a man had had a heart attack. He kicked the door down, only to discover that the guy had fallen asleep on the toilet. Sitting up straight, no less - his chin tucked on his chest, saliva drooling down his front. That was embarrassing.

Willy did what he usually does in these situations. Take advantage of the ten-inch openings that surround the door and conjoining walls. The positioning of the feet was the first give away.

Willy crouched down to his knees and tilted his head under the second cubicle's door slit. A pair of feet, as expected. But not facing him. Instead, the toes faced the left wall. The occupant's trousers hung around his ankles.

Why would anyone be standing up straight with their trousers down facing the left-hand cubicle wall.

Willy pressed his palms to the floor and lowered the side of his head millimeters from the scuzzy ground.

The occupant's underwear was taut across the guy's calves. This could only mean one thing. If it was what Willy suspected it could be, then the first cubicle would need checking.

The only problem for Willy was that his head was on its side. The blood felt like it was rushing like the contents of a lava lamp to the left of his skull.

The squelching noise appeared to intensify. Willy fell onto his hands and knees and scuttled a few inches to the left.

The first cubicle.

Willy blinked a few times as the slimy floor ground itself into his palms.

The occupant in the first cubicle shot him a dirty look. A pair of bare feet and an ass hanging between them, facing the neighboring dwelling.

The discarded shoes, socks, underwear, and jeans lay right between the man's buttocks.

Now, it was very clear what was going on. What could

Willy do in this situation?

"Yeah. You like that, Daddy?" the second cubicle moaned. It felt like the door was saying it even though the utterance was blatantly performed by a grown man.

The walls in all the cubicles seemed to knock together in unison.

Willy pushed himself from the floor and grabbed Queenie in his left hand. He wasn't going to stand for this. Not now, not here. Not in his place of work.

He banged on the first cubicle door three times.

The squelching noise stopped.

Another three bangs. No reply. Everything paused.

"Who's there?" the man in the second cubicle asked.

"Probably just some retard needing a shit," the man in the first cubicle yelled, "Hey, retard. Use one of the other shitters. This one's taken."

Willy scrunched his face and thumped the door three times once again.

"Who *is* that?" one of the men barked. It was hard to tell which one.

A screeching of rubber soles indicated that one of the men had moved away from the wall. But which one?

It didn't matter.

Willy slid his thumbnail under the first cubicle's door lock and turned it counter-clockwise.

The door jumped opened, startling the occupier - and Willy.

The man was on his knees and naked below the waist. His hand dived between his legs and rode up to his ass. Willy had a good view of the man's finger parked into his own anus.

And then, the *pènis* de résistance.

An erect and hirsute cock hung through a ten-inch hole in the middle of the wall.

The man on his knees wouldn't budge. He wasn't expecting the janitor to interrupt this feast of a blow job.

"What the hell is happening in there? Why aren't you

sucking?"

Willy had seen this glory hole charade a few times in his career. He'd never actually caught anyone red-handed, as it were. Holes were common from time to time, but this one with the penis hanging through it must have been done recently. Like, in-the-past-half-an-hour recently.

"Umm," the man on his knees shuddered and removed his finger from his asshole, "The janitor's here."

"Ah, shit," the man in the second cubicle complained. "A janitor?"

"Yeah, man."

Willy stepped into the first cubicle and grabbed the man by his collar. He lifted him to his feet and threw him out.

"Hey. What are you doing?"

Willy kicked the man's clothes out of the cubicle. He pointed at the door, indicating that the man had better leave immediately or face some pretty dire consequences.

"Has he gone yet?" the receiver in the second cubicle inquired.

The *giver* stuttered as he scrambled for his clothes and made for the door, "It's all good, D-Daddy."

Willy looked down at the glory hole and was surprised to see the erect penis still hanging through it.

"Has he gone yet?"

Willy couldn't tear his eyes away from the monster poking through the hole. Very thick, uncircumcised and around twelve inches in length. It took a good few seconds for Willy to come to terms with its enormity.

"Shit, man. You've gone quiet," the man from the other side of the wall said, "I'm going."

The erect penis jutted up and around. The slit on the crown turned to face Willy. As the man pulled himself back, the fleshy part of his penis moved several inches through the hole, forcing its foreskin over the exposed, purple head.

"Christ, I'm stuck."

Willy raised his eyebrows. *Stuck?*

The man thumped the wall twice, "Shit, shit. I can't move."

Willy released Queenie and leaned her against the toilet bowl. He knocked back on the wall twice, trying to communicate with the man.

"What the hell, man? What are you doing in there?" he screamed for dear life, "No, no. My cock is stuck."

Willy opened the fingers on his left and hand reached down to the hanging penis.

He lifted his upturned palm around the underside of the shaft. His fingers closed around it. Willy couldn't bear to watch his own action and kept his eyes shut.

"Oh, oh," the man gasped and attempted to catch his breath. He seemed to be enjoying the physical interaction, "Oh, yeah."

Willy tightened his grip on the man's penis and unraveled the toilet tissue from his right hand. He wrapped it around the appendage in the hope that his plan might set the guy free.

Around and around the paper went, building up around the shaft.

Willy threaded his thumb between the tissue paper and wall hole, trying to wedge it through.

"What are you doing?" the man panted from the other side of the wall, "Is that tissue paper?"

Willy knocked on the wall twice.

"Okay," The man moved back. His penis moved back, too, but not very far. It was still caught.

Willy shook his head and clawed away at the paper, sending shards of it to the floor.

"It's stuck," the man cried tried to shift back. The penis waved around in all directions, threatening to disappear back through the hole.

Willy had an idea. If he could somehow temper the appendage and reverse its rigidity, it would easily slip through the hole.

He clenched his left fist and bopped the head of the man's penis twice.

"Gah," the man screamed.

The penis didn't go flaccid. If anything, it grew - and stiffened. Willy clenched his fist once again and thumped on the head.

The bulbous mound of flesh bent up around the shaft, snapping the flesh underneath the crown.

The action caused the man to scream blood thunder as the penis coughed out a patch of blood down Willy's trouser leg.

An angry, repetitive thumping sounded across the dividing wall, "You b-bastard."

And then...

The erect penis slipped back through the hole, vanishing entirely. A couple of footsteps followed immediately after.

Wily gasped as he looked at the hole. The engorged member hadn't taken the skin with it. A long and droopy sheath of cream-colored skin hung around the hole like a deflated condom.

Willy bolted out of the cubicle, holding out his tissue-covered fist.

He stepped in front of the second cubicle door and slammed his fist on it. The man began to sob and whine at once.

The door opened, allowing Willy to see the result of his efforts.

A man of around fifty years of age, trousers around his ankles, nursing his skinless, erect penis. It resembled an angry, scaly snake.

The amount of blood-letting was insane.

Willy held his tissued fist over his mouth, aghast. The man looked up at him in sheer anger. He raised his finger at Willy.

"*You* did this to me."

Willy shook his head, insisting he was innocent.

"Come here, you sick faggot," the man made for Willy but tripped to the ground. His trousers were shackled around his ankles.

Willy stepped back and allowed the man to regain his composure and, hopefully, his temper.

"Come here," the man roared at Willy as he fumbled through his trouser legs and back to his feet.

The smeared gore of his freshly-torn penis bleached around the ground as he rose to his feet. The man made for Willy and threw a punch.

Willy dived out of the way and kept his tissued hand up by his face. The man hit the washbasin and pushed himself around.

He tried to attack Willy again. Raising his fist, he threw another punch. This time, it connected. The second and third knuckle on the man's bloodied fist socked Willy right in the mouth.

A rope of blood shot from his lips as he stumbled back against the urinals.

Each ceramic utility flushed one by one, thinking someone had finished using them.

The man stormed forward and towered over Willy. His bloodied penis, coughing ropes of blood left and right as he made his way toward Willy.

"You think you can get away with this, you prick?" He stood in front of Willy and placed his hands on his hips.

Willy shook his head as he pushed himself up to his feet using the urinals for balance. He held out his hand for a truce and spat a tooth to the floor.

The injured man wasn't having any of it. He raised his hand with the intention of striking Willy a final time.

Willy closed his eyes and prepared for the worst. He imagined himself dying and granted with one, final wish. All he wanted was to be set free from the clutches of this maniac.

Whatever it was, it was a distraction. A cacophony of scooshing noises erupted behind the man.

Willy opened his eyes to find that the taps on all six washbasins were on full blast. His wish had come true!

The man turned over his shoulder and tried to identify the source of the commotion, "What *is* that noise?"

It was enough time for Willy to take advantage. He raised his right hand and socked the man in the face. He yelped and stepped back, his severed penis slapping against his bare thigh.

The man turned around, puzzled, holding his jaw, "You hit me."

Willy waste no time and growled at the man. He stepped forward and kicked his assailant right between the legs.

Oof.

The man's body flew back and hit the basins, showering him with water.

"Gaahhhhhhhh."

Willy watched the man roll over the bank of washbasins, soaked in water. He screamed in pain and fell to the floor.

***

"So, let me get this straight, Mr Gee," the police officer said as he perused his notes in the office.

Willy felt around his mouth. The absence of his front tooth was getting to him.

The officer looked up and released his notes from his grip, "Are you okay?"

Willy nodded and removed his hand from his mouth. His teeth had blood smeared on them. The officer looked down and noticed the stains on on his interviewee's shirt. He looked back up to the man's blood-stained teeth once again.

The police officer looked somewhat concerned, "Are you sure you're okay?"

Willy nodded his head, insisting he was perfectly fine.

The officer shrugged his shoulders and looked at his notepad.

"Okay, so, you were inspecting the gents. You noticed two men in the cubicles. One was performing fellatio on the other?"

Willy nodded and took a napkin from his pocket.

"So, you entered the first cubicle. And the guy performing the, uh, *fellatio* ran off?"

The officer looked at Willy as he pushed the napkin under his top lip.

"The man receiving fellatio then tried to attack you in the middle of the gentlemens' convenience. At which point you defended yourself and hit him back?"

The door to the office opened, catching both the officer's and Willy's attention. An out of breath Ted moved in and closed the door behind him. He looked at Willy's face. The tissue stood out like a sore thumb.

Ted moved over to the desk for a good look at his employee, "My God, Willy. What happened?"

"It's okay, sir," the officer said, unamused at the proceedings, "I think I have everything I need."

Ted was confused. He didn't know who to address, "How do you mean? What happened—"

"—Willy, here, managed to defend himself. I don't think he realizes it yet, but he's helped us catch someone we've been after for a while, now."

"Who?" Ted asked.

"There's been reports of a man hanging around malls, public baths, that kind of thing. My colleague is surveying the CCTV right now and the suspect has been apprehended. A good turn has been done here, today."

The officer collected his notes and made for the door. Ted caught up to him.

"Thank you for your assistance, Mr Gee," the officer said. "If we need further information we'll be in touch."

Willy smiled at him. The tissue moved up his lips. Ted looked very concerned and turned to the officer.

"Actually, officer. Do you mind if we have a quick word?"

"Sure."

Ted pushed the door open and offered the officer through. The door closed gently behind them but didn't fully close

Willy was suspicious. What was it that Ted wanted to say? It had been something of a tumultuous morning. The least he deserved was a vague indication of what was going through his manager's mind.

Willy stood up from his chair and made for the wall. He eavesdropped on the two men's conversation through the crack in the door.

"—For a few weeks, now," Ted whispered to the officer, "I'm not sure you can trust everything he might have told you."

"Look, sir," the officer said. "I have the interview notes. We'll be correlating that with the evidence we get. Particularly the CCTV footage."

"Do you think this could go to court?" Ted asked.

Willy raised his eyebrows. He hadn't done anything wrong. He had merely defended himself.

"In all likelihood, yes. I'm sure we have enough evidence for the CPS—"

"—It's just that I'd rather my employee not be put under any undue stress right now."

"Why's that, sir?"

"As I said. He's recently bereaved and not in the best of health," Ted looked back through the door. He didn't spot Willy spying on them.

"Look, sir, I appreciate you having your employee's best interests at heart. It's early days yet but rest assured we'll—"

The door pulled shut, causing Willy to jump in his shoes. Ted had shut it, conscious of the fact that the conversation he was having was private.

Willy couldn't hear much more than a muffled to-and-fro between the men.

Then, a clunking noise came from the other side of the office. The side wall, with the safe. The handle had swung down.

Willy widened his eyes and hopped over it, keeping the tissue pressed against his gums.

He crouched down and lifted the handle. It had become limp.

For safety, he spun the dial around. One, one, eight. The door unbolted and swung outward.

Willy reached in and pushed the rucksack to one side. Thank God it was still there. The shadow cast onto the safe by the strip light meant that Willy had trouble seeing inside.

He reached his right hand in and felt around for the parcels Ian had given him earlier. All he needed was to feel one of them and his mind would be at rest.

He wasn't afforded the opportunity, though.

The door opened, and Ted stepped into the room. Willy closed his eyes, evidently caught red-handed.

"What are you doing there, Willy?"

Willy took a few deep breaths as Ted stood behind him. He pulled the top of the rucksack out and showed it to his manager.

"Ah, putting your stuff away, right?"

Willy nodded. He breathed a sigh of relief and turned around and shut the safe door.

His fingers pushed the dial around to a random three-digit number.

"Yeah. This is turning out to be a nightmare of a day, right?"

Willy shrugged his shoulders and grabbed the safe door handle. He gave it a good yank to ensure it was locked. The handle swung down, broken.

Willy grunted and stood back up to his feet. Checking the contents of the safe would have to wait.

Ted sat on the chair opposite the desk, "Don't think I *don't* know what's going on here, Willy."

Willy turned to stone in his shoes. He was busted. Ted knew precisely what was going on.

"Take a seat, Willy."

He did as instructed. Beads of sweat formed across his forehead. It was only a matter of moments before the police officer would return. This time, it would be to bust Willy for possession for whatever he had in the safe.

"How many years have we worked together?"

Willy shrugged his shoulders. He knew they'd worked together for a hell of a long time. A couple of decades of him working with nefarious mobsters like Ian on the side. The *front* of the whole endeavor had him chiseling skid marks off the toilet bowls. It was one hell of a convincing front if nothing else.

"I'll tell you how long. Twenty-two years, that's how long."

Willy nodded and agreed. He didn't care - he just wanted Ted out of the office.

"Why didn't you tell me what was going on? It would have made everything so much easier."

A tear rolled down Willy's calm face. He turned to the safe and held out his finger. His lips opened. He may as well confess now and get the inevitable over with.

Ted and his big mouth beat him to it.

"Your wife passes away and you're ill. You shouldn't be working."

Willy coiled his finger back into his palm. Ted knew sod all about the stuff in the safe. He felt a pang of relief he was hoping to have felt a few months when he had his biopsy results back.

"Why didn't you tell me, Willy?"

Ted's response was met with a blank stare. Willy was processing the wonderful news that he was in the clear. To Ted, it looked as if Willy was quite understandably perturbed. To have been considered a friend who knew what was *really* going on in his life.

Willy couldn't have given any less of a shit about their friendship.

"It's okay, mate," Ted took Willy's hands in his. Friend-to-friend, heart-to-heart, "I get it. I don't know for sure what it was that the hospital told you, but I know it can't have been good."

Willy was about to speak. If only Ted had shut up for ten seconds. But, no, his earnest philanthropy needed massaging a bit more before he felt he could leave.

"You don't have to tell me, Willy. I get it," Ted released his employee's hands. He stood to his feet and replaced the chair under his desk, "I'll drop the plans down to the office at the end of your shift so we can go through them.

His suggestion wasn't met with any confirmation.

"Look, Willy. If you ever need to talk you know where I am. Okay?"

Willy nodded, causing the spent tear roll off his cheek and splash to the ground. It seemed like an eternity before it hit the ground.

He gave Willy a knowing and friendly chuckle, "You'd better clean up before the punters complain," Ted tapped the side of his nose with his index finger and left the office.

The door shut behind him.

Willy let out a huge sigh of relief. A deep intake of air, followed by the loudest of exhales.

He immediately dived for the safe. His knees hit the floor. The dial couldn't be turned to one-one-eight fast enough.

The door unbolted, jutting outward. The tip of the rucksack seemed to bellow out like a lung and fall towards his lap.

Willy shoved his arm past the rucksack. He prodded his fingers around inside but couldn't find anything.

A bit more prodding... and, finally, success. He felt a sliver of plastic brush past his fingertips.

Using the safe lid for balance, he pushed the rest of his arm in and tilted his head after it.

His free arm followed it... followed by his torso, waist and then... his legs.

***

The safe door clanged shut behind Willy as he tumbled inside. It was pitch dark. He held out his hand and tried to feel around for something... *anything*.

There were two sounds that gave the impression of a vast space.

The first was his own breathing. Heightened and quickened. He didn't know where he was.

The second sound was familiar. A drip, drip, drip from a loose pipe. Water hitting *something*.

Willy put one foot forward, hoping the floor continued in front of him. It did. He trod the sole of his shoe onto the hard ground.

The other foot went forward and hit the ground.

Still utter darkness. Willy stopped and looked behind him. The thin outline of a rectangular door. White light shifted through it, illuminating the particles of dust hanging in the air.

Willy faced forward and continued walking. He made it forward around twenty steps.

The dripping sound grew louder.

His fingers brushed over something. It felt like plastic.

"What do you think you're doing?" a familiar, booming, and threatening male voice asked from high above his head.

Willy looked up. He couldn't see anything. Still, complete darkness.

"Are you trying to screw me over, Willy Gee?" the voice asked.

Willy shook his head. It wasn't as if the person asking the questions could see him, though.

"Don't mess me around, nah," the voice threatened as Willy moved his hand from the plastic, "Ya better get back to work. Here, let me help ya."

A strip of light flashed to life, illuminating the left-hand side of the room. Two gray walls and a hard ground.

The second strip of light ran across the ceiling to Willy's right. It mirrored the featureless walls and ground to the left of Willy's body.

Finally, a third strip light zipped over Willy's head, illuminating the middle.

Hundreds of rectangular parcels stared back at Willy and reached out to infinity…

A brief slash of a black man's face laughed nose-to-nose with Willy. He screamed for dear life as the face roared into his.

Willy yelped. His eyelids peeled up. The bloodied tissue fell from his gum and onto his lap.

He'd fallen asleep for a brief moment. He blinked a few times and tried to acclimatise himself to his surroundings.

He was in his office, sat on his chair in front of his desk. The light was on. The door was shut.

He turned around to the safe. Everything seemed to be in order.

How long was he out for? He remembered the police officer. Before that, the man who'd hit him.

The entire morning rewound past his brain. The speed of the images sent a crashing tornado of a migraine through his cranium.

Sparkles of white enveloped his vision as he slid off his chair and crashed to the floor, elbows-first.

"Ahhhh," Willy screamed in pain as the array of multi-colored lights panged and exploded. His eyelids snapped shut in retaliation. He kicked the chair back and thrashed around on the floor trying to make it stop.

But it wouldn't stop.

"Dad," a female whisper shot into his right ear.

The lights subsided.

Willy took a deep breath, keeping his head held in his hands. The pain dissipated, leaving Willy on his back on the floor trying to catch his breath.

A few deep breaths. His chest inflated and then he exhaled.

Willy grabbed the chair and hoisted himself to his feet. He noticed the bloodied tissue stuck to his lap. He prodded around his gum. His front tooth was still missing.

All this calamity was wearing him down. He needed to take a seat and shut his eyes for a few moments. The nightmare would soon pass.

He pressed his palm to the desktop and felt a small card. The officer's contact details.

Willy took some respite that he hadn't gone fully insane. A temporary bad dream that would only last a few minutes.

He breathed in and out, trying to calm himself down. The wall clock seeped into his field of vision: 11:56 am.

As he rested his face in his open hands, all he could hear was the tick, tick, tick from the wall clock. It felt good. Reassuring, even. The morning was coming to a close.

His manager was right, though, he thought to himself. In any other situation, he shouldn't really be working. Not now, not in his condition. He'd gotten away with it for a few weeks, but recently, it was all proving to be a much.

He certainly didn't possess the energy of the shoppers. The Kaleidoscope was full of them now that lunch was commencing.

A steady influx of prospective convenience users made their way past the office. He could tell by the level of commotion from the other side of the door.

Lunchtime. Perhaps a bite to eat would see him through the rest of the day.

Chapter 4
12:00 – 13:00

Willy stood in the middle of the gents toilets in something of a catatonic state. Lost in his own thoughts, he surveyed the area. The tissue swab that had caught most of the bloodletting had infused with his gum.

The cubicles were all empty, which was strange for the beginning of the lunchtime rush. A large man relieved himself at the first urinal.

Willy stepped forward, taking the tissue from his mouth. It tried to cling to the gum as we moved it away. The paper piece fell into the bin.

The hunt was on for his missing front tooth.

It must have landed somewhere, probably in the first cubicle or in its immediate vicinity.

It was nowhere to be found, though. A thorough scan of the floor surrounding the toilet bowl returned nothing but odd scraps of tissue paper.

A few spots of water.

A ray of light burst through the hole in the wall. Fragments of the man's skin had caked around the circle. The majority of the flap of skin had fallen to the floor. Around it, no tooth could be seen.

A quick check of the second cubicle.

On the floor, a few spots of blood. Willy crouched down and examined the area. He unwound three sheets of toilet tissue from the dispenser and cleared the splat of blood away. The substance smeared across the floor and collected into the tissue.

He dumped it into the toilet bowl and yanked down on the flush.

A slight ringing from the pipes occurred as the flush swallowed down the tissue.

The sound of a sprinkling flush came from the urinals, followed by a series of footsteps.

Willy couldn't see his tooth at all. Was it possible for it to have rolled elsewhere? Willy looked around and stood back to his feet.

He pressed his forefinger against the cavity on his mouth. A strange feeling of incompleteness fell over his back. The affront to his person felt all-too-real. A part of him was missing, and it was important that he found it.

Stepping out of the cubicle, he saw the large man washing his hands in the third washbasin.

Willy crept forward as the lines of the flooring moved past the sole of his shoes.

At the urinals, there was no tooth. In the middle section of the gents, still no success.

The large man's phone went off.

"Ugh, always when my hands are wet," he muttered to himself as he wiped off the excess water onto his blazer. The phone seemed impatient. It wanted to be answered.

"Yes. Okay, okay," he moaned as he retrieved the phone from his pocket and held it to his face, "Yes, what is it? I'm busy."

Willy kept an ear out as the conversation took place. He moved over to the washbasins, perching himself by the hand dryer.

The large man seemed very put-out with his phone call, "Yes, I know the meeting is on," he stopped himself from talking as he took some new information in, "What do you mean it's been moved?"

He threw his arm out in front of him, enabling his

sleeve to roll up his arm and reveal his wristwatch, "Twelve fifteen? It was meant to be twelve-thirty."

The large man lowered his arm and hopped over to the dryer, nodding Willy out of the way.

The man slipped the phone between his neck and ear and threw both hands under the dryer. It sprang to life, making the phone call hard to continue.

"What, yeah?" the man said as Willy stepped back and continued to watch, "I'll be there in two minutes."

Willy focused on the man's hands dancing together. Right knuckles over the left palm, and vice versa. The beads of water seemed to blow around the curvature of his hands, but not dry them.

"I can't hear you?" the man yelled down his phone, "It's twelve oh five right now."

Five past twelve, Willy thought to himself. He felt he should be somewhere, but couldn't arrive at the answer.

The hand dryer stopped blowing cold air over the man's hands as he moved away from the device, "I'm on my way." A quick check in the mirror to confirm his appearance was the last thing Willy saw of him.

The large man exited the toilet, leaving Willy alone. Still toothless.

Willy double-took and raised his eyebrows. He knew where he had to be - he'd arranged it earlier this morning.

Willy arrived at the entrance of the *Bean There, Done That* coffee store. It was right around the corner from the walkway to his office. Forty-eight steps was all it took. He found himself out of breath as he arrived.

It was now minutes after twelve. He was late.

He looked around at the hordes of shoppers moving past him and then through the window of the coffee shop. Maxine was nowhere to be seen.

Willy looked over to the information desk. The woman behind it smiled at him as she assisted a shopper. He didn't smile back, though.

He was worried that his daughter may have arrived and thought she'd been stood up. That was the last thing Willy wanted right now. It had been a long time since he saw her.

"Hey!" came a familiar voice from behind him. A hand landed on his shoulder.

Willy turned around. It was Maxine. She, too, was out of breath. He looked relieved.

"Sorry I'm late, Dad," she said. "The bus was held up."

Willy smiled and gave her a hug which took her completely by surprise, "Oh."

She clutched him in her arms and hugged him back. Willy moved his head back and examined his daughter's face. Then, he noticed many of the other shoppers doing exactly the same thing. They looked at her and smiled and seemed to ignore Willy.

It wasn't surprising. Maxine was in her early twenties and had a complexion that was enviable to most other women. Long, healthy black hair flowed down her shoulders. The formal suit completed the look. Willy was proud that she was his daughter.

she nodded at the coffee shop, "Shall we go in? I'm afraid I don't have much time."

Willy and Maxine took a booth at the far corner of the store. The drinks had already been ordered. Maxine had paid, insistent on buying lunch for her father.

Willy didn't have much to say. When did he ever? He simply smiled at her, enjoying her company.

Maxine took a sip from her glass of water and pushed the menu to one side. She was unsure if she should instigate any conversation, but threw caution to the wind.

"So, how have you been?" she asked.

Willy shrugged his shoulders and toyed with his own menu.

"It's been a year, Dad."

He nodded and agreed with her, trying to shrug off the

pain of what this fact actually meant to them.

The coffee shop got busy. Maxine and her father had arrived just before the lunch rush kick-off. A queue formed at the counter. The patrons seemed annoyed at the fact that the best seat in the place - the corner booth - was occupied already. Maxine received a few unearthly glances.

A couple ordered their two children to take a seat near the window.

"Have you got nothing to say?" Maxine asked in an attempt to tear his attention away from the line.

He looked back and then down to his hands. Maxine placed her water on the table and looked at her father.

"Look, it's been difficult for all of us. I just wanted to chip the ice, you know. There's no point in denying it happened. No point in pretending it doesn't affect us."

Willy nodded once again. He pressed his right hand under his left arm and winced.

"Is that blood on your lip?" Maxine asked, taken aback by her discovery - it was *definitely* blood around his mouth.

Willy wouldn't look up from his hands. Maxine reached over and tucked her knuckle under his chin and tilted his head up. Her eyes widened.

"My God, that *is* blood?" she reached over to the napkin holder, "Hang on."

She took out a single sheet of tissue and wet it with her tongue, "Here,"

She wiped the blood spot from his top lip and folded the tissue in half, "What happened?"

Willy pressed his top lip up with his thumb and revealed his missing front tooth.

"Oh," Maxine held her face with her hands in surprise, "Did you get into a fight or something?"

Willy paused for a moment and then nodded his head.

"Jesus, you need to go to the dentist. Did this just happen?"

He looked down and half-smiled. Maxine was very unimpressed with her father's behavior. She couldn't contain her displeasure.

"You know, if you want to meet up with me for a chat, then the least you can do is—"

The barista arrived at the table with a tray of drinks and food, "Okay. We have the ham salad?"

Maxine looked up, "Oh yes. That's for me," She took the plate from the barista. He looked down at the ticket on the tray and continued, "And the double espresso?"

"Yep. Mine, too. Thanks."

He placed the drink in front of her and looked at Willy, "So, you must be the black Americano."

He set Willy's drink in front of him. "That's great. Anything else?"

"No thanks," Maxine threw the guy a polite smile that seemed to say *"go away"*.

"Have a great day, then," the barista ran off back to the counter, leaving Maxine and Willy alone.

She took the sugar packet and tore off the end, "You sure you don't want anything to eat?"

Willy didn't respond. He was too busy staring at the tabletop. Maxine poured half of the contents into her drink and stirred it with the spoon.

Willy slid his coffee into his other palm. He didn't put anything in the drink but still stirred it with his spoon.

The vortex of bubbles swirled around and around. Willy seemed fixated with the pattern.

Maxine thumped the table, uneasy with her father's mute behavior. The violent action caused an almighty racket, "Well, *okay then*."

Willy looked up. Everyone else in the place looked over at them, somewhat startled.

Maxine didn't care much, though. She was more preoccupied with her father's refusal to contribute to the conversation.

"One *whole* year," she began to well up, "Don't you give a shit?"

"I'm sick, Maxine," Willy blurted for the first time

today. A gravelly, disheveled voice of a man who, indeed, was not well.

"Sick?" Maxine asked. "What do you mean sick?"

"How long has it been since we last saw each other?"

Maxine sighed and wiped a tear from her eyes, "Mum's funeral."

"Yes."

Now it was Maxine's turn to avoid the truth and her father's gaze, "What do you mean you're *sick*?"

She didn't want to know the truth. In fact, she didn't want an answer other than *"haha, just kidding!"* from her father.

But she knew that wouldn't be happening today. Willy wasn't known for his sense of humor. He wasn't about to reveal that he'd developed one in the past twelve months.

"The doctor gave me three months six months ago."

Maxine's spoon slipped out of her fingers and clanged to the table top. She'd been dreading this news. Her face never lifted. In a curious turn of events, she was now the one who'd be going quiet.

"What," she failed to choke back her tears, "What is it?" she held her head in her hand and closed her eyes, "Just tell me."

"It's, uh, spread into the lymph nodes. It's not good."

Maxine left a ten-second pause. A million questions tumbled around in her head like a fruit machine. One eventually landed that needed asking immediately.

"I knew something was up. I just didn't know what," she looked up at him and sniffed back the phlegm that had built up in her sinuses, "I knew it."

"I'm sorry, Max."

"Why didn't you tell me?"

Willy hung his head in shame, "I didn't want to worry you."

"Worry me?" she half-chuckled with despair, "What, did you think I was going to find out?"

"No, of course not, but—"

"—And you keep it to yourself?" Maxine looked at her salad. She slid it across the table away from her, "Ugh."

Willy tried to smile with as much affection as he could muster. "I'm sorry."

"You didn't take any treatment? No chemo, no medicine?"

"No."

"Why not?"

"No point. It was too late. I just didn't want to be helpless and sick," Willy revealed. "In some funny way, maybe, if I just buried my neck in my work, perhaps it would just all go away."

Maxine burst out laughing through her tears, "Are you kidding me right now?"

"Not really, no."

"You think you can just run and hide from—" Maxine stopped herself and swallowed hard. She noticed he was checking her salad out, "Are you hungry?"

"A bit, yes."

Maxine bit her lip and placed her hand on the plate. He looked back at her, a grin streaking across his lips. She pushed the salad toward him.

"Help yourself."

"Thanks."

He took a fork, dug into the lettuce and shoveled it into his mouth, "Mmmm."

Maxine stared at her father. He must have been ravenous. He munched away in his own little world at such an alarming rate.

"Good?"

Willy nodded and approved the food with the prongs on his fork.

"Missing tooth not setting you back?" she chuckled.

"Nuh-huh," he said with a mouthful of food.

Maxine looked out of the booth and saw a few of the patrons looking back at them, "What are you looking at?" she scowled.

They all turned around and looked back at their phones, pretending not to have seen anything.

"Unbelievable," she muttered to herself as Willy guzzled his food down. She turned to face him, "Aren't you in any pain?"

"I'm self-medicating," he said and wiped the salad dressing from his bottom lip.

"Self-medicating?" Maxine instantly realized that her father had slipped back to his old ways. A wave of disappointment fell across her face, "Oh. *Right*."

Willy scooped up the rest of the salad and threw it into his mouth.

"So, you know better than the doctors, right? I can't believe this."

"What do you mean?"

"You're not fit for work."

"I'm fine."

"It hasn't affected your appetite, evidently," she nodded at the empty bowl and watched her father guzzle down his coffee in one hit. He slammed the cup onto the saucer and gasped for air.

"Okay, that's enough," she snapped. "What time does your shift finish today?"

"What?" Willy wiped his mouth with a napkin.

"Your shift. Today. What time are you clocking off?"

"Oh, uh. Six. It's late night shopping."

"Does your boss know?"

"Yes," Willy took the opportunity to lighten the mood, "He knows Thursday is late night shopping."

"Don't get funny with me, Dad," she barked. "I mean does he know you're not well?"

"Uh, no," Willy hushed. "Not exactly."

"*Not exactly?*" Maxine looked at her wristwatch and thought aloud, "I'm going to give him a call and we'll meet him after work and explain—"

"—No," Willy snatched her wrist and yanked her forward, "Don't do that."

"What?"

"Don't tell him. *Please*."

"Dad, you're unwell," Maxine quipped. "You can't work. You can stay with me. We need to sort stuff out."

"No, Max. It's all taken care of," he kept her wrist tight in his grip. There was no way he'd allow her to ruin his plan, "Please, Max. Do this for me."

Maxine shook his hand away from her wrist and folded her arms, "Let go of me."

She teared up as the news finally sunk in. Willy exhaled and became remorseful in an instant, "Honey, please."

There she sat, bawling her eyes out over her untouched coffee in full view of the coffee shop patrons. Willy sympathized, of course. The ignominy was hard to deal with in full view of complete strangers.

"I should have told you when I knew."

"You w-weren't g-going to t-tell me. Were you?"

Willy looked at his hands and shook his head, "No."

Maxine kicked the table leg in anger, "I can't believe you, sometimes," she wiped the tears from her cheek and slid out from the booth.

"Where are you going?"

"I need to be alone for a while," she rose to her feet and picked her handbag up from the seat, "You weren't going to tell me. After what happened with mom, I just. I just—"

It was all too much. She ran out of the coffee store bawling like a little girl.

Willy was alone at the booth. Time enough to reflect on the emotional damage he'd inadvertently inflicted on his last remaining relative.

The harsh sun beat down on the entrance to the Kaleidoscope. It was blinding and fierce, unseasonably hot. The schools had started their new academic term. As a result the mall was less busy during the day.

Even so, Willy found some comfort in the warmth

enveloping his face as he held his head up to the sky with his eyes closed.

In his hands, he rolled up the next joint for the day. The one that might see him through his shift with the least amount of pain.

He ran the paper along the tip of his tongue and pressed the wet ends together, keeping an eye on his surroundings.

The fountain operated at full pelt, shooting water in a diamond formation from its exit holes. The water splashed against some youngsters playing around in the stone moat.

A couple of mothers chatted away at each other, neither of them listening to what the other had to say.

A shopkeeper enjoyed a cigarette, perched on the edge of the bench.

Next to him, that elderly woman with the gold earring was still there. He gave her a smile. She closed her eyes and nodded, reaching into her inside coat pocket for something.

Willy inserted the roach into the end of his joint and closed the paper around it. It darted between his lips and was met by a naked flame.

He sucked down on his first draw. The smoke funneled down his throat and split into a fork as it entered his lungs.

It felt good. A wave of tingly heaven massaged his body. The pain dissipated.

He opened his eyes as slow as he could and then exhaled. The plume of white smoke enveloped his vision temporarily. As the cloud moved away, it revealed the elderly woman on the bench a few feet away from him.

She lay on her side. Her bag dropped to the floor. Was she taking a nap, Willy wondered as he took a second, deep drag from his joint.

Who could blame her? It wasn't against the law to make yourself comfortable, no matter how indignant lying on a bench may appear to the other shoppers.

The bag hitting the floor was the giveaway to Willy, as

he felt his muscles ground to a halt.

The shopkeeper looked over his shoulder and spotted the woman lying down. He jumped from his seat and turned to her.

"Oh God," he reacted in super-slow motion, "Are you feeling okay, my love?"

The outer edges of the man's contours seem to drift and try to catch up as he scrambled to his knees to assist the elderly lady. Something wasn't right.

Even the two mothers looked over as a few exiting shoppers stopped to watch.

The shopkeeper stood up and took a few steps back, unsure what to do. He took out his phone.

Willy held out his hand as everything he saw slowed down to half-speed. "No, no," his voice falling on deaf ears, "Sh-she needs help."

Willy tried to stand but struggled to keep his balance. The joint had done its job tenfold.

He watched the elderly woman roll off the bench and hit the ground, staring obliquely into the sky. The gold earring slumped against the ground.

Willy turned to the shopkeeper and tried to assist. But he couldn't move.

The man took a picture of the elderly woman on the floor. The two mothers gasped in terror and stepped back away from the commotion.

"What," Willy muttered with disbelief under his breath, his speech just making its way past his lip,. "Wh-hy is no-one h-helping?"

One of the mothers called her child over from the fountain. The other woman took out her phone. Thank God, it seemed someone was calling an ambulance.

Willy patted his pocket and remembered he had left his phone in the office. The woman turned her phone sideways and filmed the elderly woman on the floor.

Stone, silent. Very dead.

Half of the shoppers ignored the old bird completely

and went about their day. The drifting haze of their presence glowed brightly as they zoomed past Willy's field of vision.

The ones who didn't stop to help moved toward the main road at speed. The ones who weren't moving simply pointed and muttered at the old lady.

They didn't seem to register the upper half of her body rattling on the ground from left to right.

"C-Can't you s-see?" Willy attempted to shout at the shopkeeper and anyone who was close enough to listen, "L-Look."

The elderly lady's shoulders buckled upward. A tear in her coat burst through the seams and ran down to her waist.

Willy's face was one of shock. What happened next was almost immediate and completely unexpected.

Two giant wings shot out from under her back and spread across the ground. At least five feet wide, white and feathery. The action didn't perturb anyone watching other than Willy.

Not least when the pair of wings came to life and began to jump and hammer the floor.

"Oh n-no," Willy dropped the joint on the ground and blinked as hard as he could, "Sh-she's going—"

The elderly lady sat up straight. Her ass lifted from the floor, dragging her feet as the wings flapped up and down. The motions were violent.

Willy looked up and observed the dead woman being carried into the sky. Why, then, was everyone else looking down at the ground where she had fallen?

"Can't you see this?" Willy screamed at the others. His voice became warbled and inaudible. No-one responded. They kept on looking at the ground.

But not Willy. He could see the truth. The woman's wings flapped like a giant hawk and carried her dead body toward the sun, disappearing out of view.

"Can anyone see me?" Willy screamed at the top of his

marijuana-fueled lungs. A blade of smoke plumed from his lips and drifted into the sky.

Willy staggered through one set of double doors that led into the Kaleidoscope. The glass ceiling above his head allowed the sunshine into the main concourse.

The light seemed to bounce against every conceivable object and into Willy's retinas. It was almost blinding. A yellow and green hue washed over his vision. With each step he took, an array of multicolored, ricocheting light smashed him against the face.

From the jewelery store, the diamonds emitted silver streak of daggers.

The reflective doors bounced back a sharp, orange beam.

Blues and greens bounced off the twenty-foot-high tubular kaleidoscope that sat in the middle of the concourse.

The blond assistant at the information desk spotted Willy struggling with his face. He pressed his palms around, sweating profusely.

"Jesus Christ," she darted out from the booth and ran over to him. She caught him in her arms and sat him down on the cold, hard floor amid some concerned onlookers.

"Willy, are you okay?"

His ass hit the cold ground with a violent thud. He groaned to himself and rubbed his forehead, "I'm okay, I'm okay."

He opened his eyes and clocked a name badge pinned to her lapel, "Rose."

She pushed him back by his chest, enabling him to rest against the tiled wall, "Do you want me to call first aid?"

"No, no," he coughed. "I'll be fine... *Rose?*"

"Yes, are you sure you're okay?" Rose turned to another assistant at the information desk and clicked her fingers, "I can get you a cup of water or something?"

"No, please," he whispered. "Just a bit of a dizzy spell,

I'll be fine in a moment or two. Thanks."

A small crowd of onlookers sighed to themselves. They went about their business. There was nothing more to see.

"Here, I'll help you up," Rose stood to her feet and offered him her left hand.

"Thanks."

He pulled himself up and brushed himself down. The stains from his vomiting session earlier in the morning had turned from a nasty yellow into a pungent and dark orange.

"Bet you've seen better days?" Rose smiled.

"Yeah. You could say that."

"I can call Mr Bundy and let him know you're unwell—"

"—No, it's okay. We're one down in convenience as it is," Willy interrupted.

Rose didn't seem so sure, "Well, okay, if you insist."

Willy took a step forward. He didn't reveal it, but his head was pounding like mad, "Thanks. Maybe I'll just take a couple headache pills or whatever."

"Look, if you're not feeling any better, please come and see me. Okay?"

"I will."

Rose gave him a smile as he trundled off toward the walkway that would take him back to his office.

"Oh, by the way," she hollered after him.

He turned around and raised his eyebrows, "Yes?"

"It's nice to finally hear your voice."

"Ha. Thanks," he chuckled to himself and ran his hand through his hair.

Willy shuffled down the walkway, toward his place of work. A three-year-old rode on the pink elephant, sitting on the blue harness.

"Mommy, look at me," the kid screamed his high-pitch voice through Willy's brain. The giggling didn't help matters, either, adding salt to an already abrasive audio wound.

A soft melodic clanging of metal wound its way along the walls as Willy kept on walking. The lights of the signage beamed with an extreme intensity.

The kid's mother fiddled with her phone while she waited for her son to stop riding that annoying elephant. The music that accompanied the ride was catchy but annoying. Like a perverse version of *Twinkle Twinkle Little Star*.

"Everyone loves riding me!" said the tinny childish narration through the speakers below the coin box. The elephant's eyes were painted dead-on, which meant that they followed you wherever you were in the room.

This was a corridor. An unearthly and somewhat delirious notion for Willy that the damn ride was looking at him. Bouncing back and forth to that interminable music. The catch phrase was the last thing he needed to hear.

After a few more steps, the ghastly device was out of view. Willy turned the corner by the repaired vending machine and entered his office.

"I swear to God I am going insane," Willy muttered and held his head in his hands. He massaged his jowls in his palms. Around and around they went, squeezing droplets of water from his eyes as his cheeks pushed up in his hands.

He looked at the picture of him, his wife, and the young Maxine on his desk. Happier times.

Maxine was only ten years old when the picture was taken. Willy and his wife were very happy back then. The beginnings of a small but happy family life. Both mum and dad had a full bill of health, too.

Willy closed his eyes and leaned back in his chair.

One Year Ago to the Day.

A croaking sound occurred around the hinges of the door as it opened. Willy walked through it and into the kitchen. He'd heard a sobbing noise coming from the room for the past half an hour. He thought it might have been the radio.

Instead, his worst fear had presented itself. An event twelve years in the coming.

His wife, Nannie, rested against the wall with her hands behind her back. She cried and went berserk.

Willy switched on the light and spotted fresh, wet blood streaks on the wall beside her waist.

"Nannie?" Willy yelped and ran over to her, "What's going on, what's wrong?"

He took her by the shoulders, hoping she'd fall into his arms and tell him her woes.

She didn't. Nannie kept crying floods of tears.

"I—know—wh-what you... *did*."

"What?" Willy shook her by the shoulders and lost his temper, "What are you talking about?"

Nannie looked at the door. Maxine peered through it, utterly concerned.

Willy looked over his shoulder. "Max, not now!"

"Is Mum okay?"

Nannie kept crying, unable to speak. Willy was insistent. "Please, Max, I got this. Just go to your room."

Maxine ran off and up the stairs. Willy turned to his wife and tried to calm her down.

"Nannie-may, please, tell me what—"

"—Get away from me," she nudged him forward in sheer rage, "Don't you dare touch me."

"Why?" he begged. "What did I do?"

"You know what you did."

"No, I don't. Please, tell me what you think it is that I did?"

Nannie kept on crying and shook her head, "Don't treat me like an idiot."

"I'm not," he protested and attempted to approach her.

"Don't come anywhere near me, you *monster*."

"Tell me what you think I did?"

"Ugh," she muttered under her breath and tried to stop wailing, "I knew it. I knew along it was you, but I wanted to believe—"

"—Tell me what I did," Willy lost his patience. He could feel his right hand clench into a fist. He didn't intend to strike his wife, but she was behaving very odd. Even for her.

"I hate you," was the only response he got.

Willy tried to calm himself down. In his mind, if he was calm it would inspire her to follow suit, "I can't do anything unless you tell me what it is you think I've done."

Nannie coughed and gasped for air. Her head withered slightly, "I've taken care of it."

"Taken care of what?" A wave of anxiety fell across Willy's soul, "What are you talking—"

Nannie looked at the kitchen counter. A large, serrated kitchen knife lay across it covered in blood.

Willy looked at it and then back to his wife. Her arms were still tucked behind her back.

The blood smeared on the wall.

Willy put two and two together, "No, no," he dived over to her as she cried even harder.

He grabbed the sides of her upper arms and tried to wrench them forward. She retaliated and shook him back.

"Get off me," she wailed.

"No, no. Show me your arms."

"Get off of me," she bawled and lost her balance - and, to an extent, her sanity. Willy kept on with her, trying to get her to release her arms.

In the fray, her knees buckled. Her cries all but stopped as she slid down the wall and crumpled to her feet in a hollowed hump.

"Nannie, I swear to God. Show me your arms."

Eventually, he managed to pull them out from behind

her back. He gasped as he turned them up.

A long, deep cut from the wrist to the elbow on each arm. She'd used blade knife to open up her veins.

The blood on the wall was a testament to her suicide attempt. A batch of it seeped down from where she'd been standing and trailed down behind her.

Nannie's head fell to the side as she lost consciousness.

"Oh, Jesus Christ," Willy roared and squeezed his grip on her hands. The blood-letting was furious, dripping down her thighs and pooling around her legs, "No, Nannie."

He grabbed her two wrists in one hand and tapped the side of her face with the other. "Nannie, can you hear me?"

No response. Out cold.

"Nannie," Willy screamed again to no response. Looking at the amount of blood she'd lost, he was certain she'd cut herself at least twenty minutes ago.

Willy turned to the kitchen door, "Maxine. Maxine," he screamed to a rumble of footsteps hurtling down the staircase.

Maxine reached the kitchen door and froze solid, "Mom?"

"She's cut herself. Call an ambulance, quick."

Maxine squealed and nearly lost her footing. She reached into her pocket, took out her phone and dialed 999. "What do we do till they get here?"

"I dunno, I dunno," Willy spat. "Should I keep her arms held up? There's blood everywhere."

"How should I know?" Maxine tucked her phone between her neck and shoulder and pulled open a kitchen drawer.

"Hello? Yes. I need an ambulance, quick." She took out a couple of tea towels and launched them at her father, "Here. Wrap them around each arm. It'll stop the blood."

Willy caught the two towels. He wrapped one of them tightly around Nannie's left wrist.

The upper half of her body slid over and crashed to the floor. Willy caught her head in his hands.

"I dunno," Maxine shouted into the phone, "I am being calm. She's cut herself and there's blood everywhere."

"Jesus, Nannie," Willy wrapped the towel around his wife's bloodied arms and tied them as best he could, "What have you done?"

Maxine paced around, "What do I do? Tell me what I do? We're wrapping her arms with towels!"

Willy secured the second towel around Nannie's right arm. The immediacy of the situation finally got the better of him, "Baby, can you hear me?"

"Twenty minutes, are you joking me," Maxine screamed down the phone at the operator, "I *am* calm, you stupid bitch. Twenty minutes is too long. She'll be dead in five."

Willy felt his wife's neck. A string of saliva roped from her mouth and collected against the floor. Her eyes remained stark and opened. Staring at her husband. Behind the glare, no-one seemed to be present.

Willy pushed his fingers into her neck once again, feeling around for a pulse. His eyes settled on hers. Her body went limp in his hands.

He knew it was over.

"I am calm, I am calm," Maxine burst into tears as she shouted at her phone, "We just need someone here right now."

Willy closed his mouth and gently released his wife's head to the ground.

He sat with his back against the wall next to his dead wife, "Maxine…"

"Hold on Dad, they're sending someone out," Maxine turned away from him and continued with the call.

"Maxine," he tried again, this time louder.

"No, Dad. Not yet. They're saying twenty—"

"—Maxine!" he shouted at the top of his lungs, "It's over. That's it. She's gone."

Maxine lowered the phone, but she wouldn't turn around. She remained standing, but utterly despondent.

"Honey."

The phone slid out of her hand and smashed against the tiled floor. Maxine didn't respond. All Willy could see was the back of his daughter standing ten feet away from him, facing the door.

"Hello, caller?" the emergency operator's voice came through the phone speaker, "Caller, are you still there?"

Chapter 5

13:00 – 14:00

Willy opened his eyes in a haze of confusion. For a second he didn't know where he was. Everything he could see was sideways. The cupboards and the wall clock were all tilted. Even the stock cupboard door.

He blinked and tried to lift his head. Every time he moved his shoulders up, a sharp pain shot through his brain.

"Ugh," he exhaled as loud as possible. His breath pushed some white powder along the table and into view. He looked down, startled, and pushed himself up straight against the chair.

He was at his desk. White powder lay all over the top of his desk. Next to it was one of the gold parcels Ian had left for him earlier this morning. Willy had no idea how it had got out.

A slit was present along the side of the parcel. It must have been the key on his bunch that rested atop the table that did it. The powdered contents were spilling out through the deep tear.

"Oh no, no," Willy grabbed the bunch of keys and flipped to the gold one. He blew the powder from it and set about scooping the white stuff with the side of his hand. "Shit, shit…"

As he bent over the table and collected it all up, a drop of blood hit the middle of it.

Then another. And another.

Willy held his finger up to his nose. It was bleeding quite badly. The red droplets mixed in with the powder, turning into a muggy, congealed mess.

Willy examined his finger and noticed more powder on it. The reflection in the family picture returned his image. Above his wife's smiling face, Willy started back at himself. A diluted, hazy image of what had happened.

The blood wouldn't stop dripping. The red stuff added to the concoction of stains that already adorned his shirt. Quick -thinking, he turned his hand up and pressed the fleshy part of his thumb against his left nostril.

He stood up out of his chair and almost lost his balance. The effect of the powder was clearly taking effect. A bad combination of a high and lack of sleep, he tumbled backward and booted the chair backward.

It slammed against the safe, knocking against the open door.

Willy looked down in sheer confusion. He hadn't opened the safe. He didn't remember taking any of the contents out at all. One thing was for certain, though. He'd need to get the parcel back in there and locked. He hoped that no-one, not least Ian, would suspect he'd broken into one of the packages.

Willy darted over to the stock cupboard and pulled the door open.

The white light snapped on, illuminating the dark and dusty dwelling. Shelves upon shelves of cleaning products lined the walls.

Bleach, detergent, wet wipes, toilet rolls, and replacement parts for some of the utilities that were in the toilets.

Last, a packet of hand tissues.

Willy tore out a box of tissues from the cellophane wrapper and lifted the perforated edge. In any other situation this would have been an easy maneuver. Still plugging his bleeding nose, trying to open it one-handed was a damn nightmare.

The box dropped toward the floor and hit his foot. He bent over to pick it up.

A quick glance at the shelves revealed that nothing was unwrapped. It was either use both hands or struggle for an inordinate amount of time with just the one.

Willy lifted up his shirt around his waist and released his thumb from his nostril. After all, it was already bloodied. What damage could a few more spots do in the time it would take to stuff it up his nose and clog the flow?

He wrapped the loose end of his undershirt around his thumb and shoved it into his nose. The blood flow was relentless. At least his shirt's fabric had soaked it all up. It gave him time enough to grab the tissue box with both hands and tear it open in haste.

"Come on, *come on*," he struggled with the box as it seemed to grow in his hands, "Come *on*."

Willy slid his index finger inelegantly through the perforation. He yanked it apart and tore the top away. A bunch of tissue jutted out through the tear.

All the blood loss played furiously with his sense of balance. He stepped backward and tore a tissue from the box as it left his clutches and fell, once again, to the floor.

Out came his shirt. So, too, did a string of congealed red phlegm. Like a burst artery, it roped from his nostril and splatted down his front. The image repulsed Willy. He was never happy with the sight of blood. His elbow knocked the shelf, causing the row of bleach bottles to wobble perilously on the spot. It gave him enough time to fashion a small bullet from the tissue paper and thrust it up his nostril.

Done, crisis over. All he needed to do now was clear up the powder from the desk.

Willy marched back into the office and scooped up as much of the white powder with the side of his hand. He lay the split-end of the parcel against the picture frame and dropped the powder through the slit. Much of it was returned into the parcel.

What Willy hadn't accounted for was just how much of this stuff had whizzed up his nose. If, indeed, it had ended up there. The light from the ceiling seemed to breathe in and out as the room began to spin. Had he lost balance because of his bleeding nose? The white powder? Perhaps it was a mixture of both.

Leaving aside the blood-infused section of the grains of white stuff, the rest of the contents were returned to the parcel. It wasn't good enough, though. The parcel certainly looked like it had been opened and used.

He ran back into the stockroom with the tissue hanging out of his nose. It used to be white, but the blood had seeped right through and turned most of it red.

He looked for something specific. Anything white and crumbly. There was the bleach, once again. The toilet rolls might suffice if he could stuff them in to give the impression that the parcel was full.

Then, he hit on something. Bicarbonate of soda. Bingo.

He tore off the plastic seal, spun the lid counter-clockwise and walked back into the office.

The parcel's slit looked like a mouth, begging for a feeding. Willy hung his chest over the top of it and patted out white soda dust through the lips of the plastic.

It worked. The bicarbonate of soda filled up to the brim.

He blew the excess granules away and picked away at a piece of masking tape from the other end of the parcel. Stubborn and rigid, it needed more than his trusty thumbnail.

He lifted the parcel, slit facing the ceiling, and tore off the dangling tape end with his remaining front tooth.

Willy taped the slit over the parcel and chucked it into the safe.

The safe door slammed shut right behind it.

Convenience

Willy clutched Queenie against his chest as he moved past the baby changing facility. There didn't seem to be anyone in there. He checked his wristwatch. 1:15 pm. This was the post-lunch rush hour. An hour's worth of punters flooding in and using the facilities. God alone knew what kind of state the toilets would be in.

As Willy approached the gents toilet door a man wearing jeans made eyes at him, disgusted by what he saw: a janitor with bloodied tissue hanging from his nose, his outfit covered in all sorts of colorful stains.

"Ugh. *Mate*," the man said as he slipped past Willy, "You wanna get your outfit changed."

Willy nodded at the man, agreeing with him. "Yeah. It's laundry day."

"Whatever," the man didn't care and made his way out of the area.

"Everyone loves to ride me," a squeaky child-like voice exclaimed with glee. It came from the elephant ride in the middle of the walkway. Willy turned around to see who was riding it.

A tiny toddler enjoyed himself as the machine rocked back and forth to the tinny nursery rhyme that had haunted Willy ever since it was installed three years ago.

He sighed to himself and shook his head. Hopefully the kids might vandalize that dastardly ride instead of the vending machine on day.

He pushed the door to the gents open and walked in.

What a state. The place hummed of piss and diarrhea. A strong smell of detergent crept around the room. The place hadn't been cleaned in any meaningful way since yesterday. Somehow, the chemicals used were still hanging in the air.

Puddles of orange pee lined the tiled floor underneath the urinals.

Two businessmen were in mid-conversation, taking a

washbasin each.

Willy stepped forward, his mind racing a mile a minute. The two men appeared to be speaking in a high pitch tone and at such an alarming speed. It disturbed Willy. He did his best to mentally block out the noise. He walked over to the plastic bucket of water that had been sitting in the corner since yesterday.

Queenie's mop head dunked into the rinser and twisted around. As Willy cleaned her out, he decided how best to attack the urine puddles in front of him.

"Look, it's okay," the businessman on the left said as he splashed some water on his face, "We'll just go in there and do the presentation. I'll field the question-and-answer session. Don't worry."

"Christ, I hate these bloody things," the other man squirted some soap into his hands, "I just freeze up."

"Don't worry about it, Manny," the first man reassured his friend. "Let the slides speak for themselves. I'll take the questions. All you have to do is introduce slide two and three and leave the rest to me."

"Okay, cool. Cool." Manny held his hands under the tap and cleansed them thoroughly, "What time are we on, Trey?"

Trey, the first businessman checked his watch, "Half one. We got about ten minutes till we're on."

Manny patted himself down, "Ugh. I hate this."

Willy mopped up the urine puddle from under the first two urinals. He slid Queenie's head back and plunged the mucky bristles into the plastic bucket. A tight squeeze shifted the liquid from the heavy, soaked head.

"Here," Trey turned to Manny and took out a small, plastic bullet, "You want some of this? Take the edge off?"

Manny looked at the plastic device as Trey slipped the lid open. He patted out the contents next to his basin.

"Just a bit of speed. Nothing to worry about."

"Yeah," Manny decided. "Go on, then."

Willy slapped Queenie's head to the floor and kept

mopping. Trey looked into the mirror and saw that they had company. He turned around to Willy as Manny lowered himself and held one of his nostrils shut.

"Jesus, where did you come from?" Trey asked Willy.

"I work here," he barked back and leaned to his side, catching what Manny was doing. "What is that stuff?"

"Just a bit of speed, man," Trey giggled and snorted some of the powder from his thumb, "You want a taste?"

Willy shook his head and continued to mop the floor as the two businessmen rubbed their noses with their knuckles. Trey leaned in and whispered something to Manny.

"Can you t-take that outside, please?"

"Hey, *janitor*," Trey chuckled and pointed at Willy's bloodied tissue hanging from his nostril, "Looks like you've been at the funny marching powder yourself."

Willy reached up and felt for the tissue. He had completely forgotten it was there. He tore it from his nose and dropped it into the waste bin next to the urinal.

"I had a nose bleed," Willy blinked and snorted a length of phlegm down his throat, "It's cleared up now."

Manny stood up straight and snorted the last of the speed up his nose. He looked at Willy and laughed like a maniac at the mess of a janitor standing before him, "You look like shit, mate."

"Someone's been through the wars, haven't they?" Trey added.

Before Willy had a chance to respond, the door to the gents burst open. An overweight man waddled in as quickly as he could, unfastening his jeans belt, "Oh God, oh God."

Willy and the two businessmen watched on as the man waddled forward. He seemed to be in great turmoil as he raced toward the cubicles.

"Move, move," he seemed to be angry at his bulbous stomach overhang. It blocked his ability to unfasten the belt around his jeans.

"Whoa, big man," Trey giggled as everyone's head turned right to left, following the man into the second cubicle.

The overweight man rolled his jeans down to his ankles and jumped into the cubicle backward. He kicked the door shut. It smashed against the frame and bounced back in.

"Seems someone's in desperate need of a shit."

"Shut up," screamed the man from within the cubicle. The disgusting sound of fat whale blubber splashing into the toilet bowl echoed through the room.

Then, the undeniable sound of said whale blubber blasting out a tonne of shit from its bowels.

"Ahhh," the fat man groaned from within the cubicle amid the bubbles and farts of emanating from his frenzy of shit, "Yeah. That's the bastard shifted."

Willy moved forward, blinking his eyes over and over again. By now, he was sure the white stuff he'd taken was a reality. All of his senses heightened on the spot.

The tittering from the two businessmen.

His own footsteps against the tiled floor as he moved forward.

The shit-blasting from the fat man in the second cubicle. Every single pocket of bowel-air escaped through the guy's asshole. The sounds of flatulence stabbed Willy in the brain.

The room felt as if it was levitating and beginning to spin counter-clockwise. Willy lost his footing, slightly.

"Whoa, dude," Trey said. "Are you sure you're okay?"

Willy nodded and pressed himself against the side of the first cubicle. "Yes, I'm—"

Another putrid, fart-laden stream of shit sounded around the toilets. The unmistakable stench of the fat man's guts hung in the air.

"Oh, *shit*," Manny pointed at the entrance to the second cubicle. The interminable sound of shit blasting into the bowl was puke-inducing, "Look at *that*."

Willy looked down and saw a spread of yellow diarrhea

seep out from under the door to the cubicle.

"Hey," Willy screamed, his voice several seconds in front of his moving lips. "What's going on in there?"

"I d-don't f-feel very well," the fat man's voice barreled from the cubicle.

Trey and Manny returned to their lines of speed along the washbasins, "Good luck with that."

Willy moved in front of the second cubicle and caught the commotion in full view. The fat man had managed to kick off his jeans and shoes and had both feet on the toilet seat. Squatting down, his ungainly, opened ass cheeks hung over the bowl. The man held himself on position by placing both hands on each wall.

"Ughhhh."

Willy raised his eyebrows. The fat blancmange of human squeezed his bowels and shot a torrent of liquid shit into the pan. The water splashed back up and covered his fat-folded groin.

He lifted his head to the ceiling and screamed sheer murder, "Shit. Shit."

Willy couldn't look away. With each attempt to shit out more of his guts, the man's stomach deflated and sunk into his body.

"Oh, Christ. Help me."

"What the hell did you eat?" Willy gasped to himself as the man clenched his muscles and fired a jet of liquid yellow diarrhea into the bowl. The fat man's cheeks sunk into his face as the water splashed up and around his body.

The bowl overflowed with gooey, orange excrement. Much of it slopped to the floor and treacled in amongst the tiles, seeping toward Willy's feet.

"Sir, please stop," Willy yelled as the two businessmen chuckled at his predicament.

"That's one hell of a clean-up job you got on your hands there, mate," Trey giggled and snorted another line of speed. "Ugh, the stench of abysmal."

"Christ," the fat man released yet another jet of liquid

shit toward the u-bend. His jet of warm liquid shit pushed the already-filled contents over the lip of the seat. The excrement slopped to the ground.

Willy stepped back and threatened the man, "Stop doing that."

The fat man's face became gaunt as his double-chin sunk into his chest, "I c-can't st-stop."

"That's enough," Willy shunted Queenie's head to the floor and pressed the sole of his shoe over the bristles, "You're out of here."

He twisted the handle around and around. The metal housing twisted clockwise, sliding through the screw teeth. Willy lifted the wooden handle and held it out in front of him.

"Stop it."

The man reached under his waist and clutched one buttock in each hand and spread his asshole wide open, "Gahhh."

Yet *another* jet of orange shit fired from his guts and into the bowl. Willy roared and ran forward, lifting the headless mop to his chest.

He stabbed the man in the stomach with the fat end. It prodded into his flesh and rebounded back against the blubber. It caused the man to release his bowels once again.

"Get away," screamed the man.

"No," Willy hoisted the weapon above his head, "Get out of here. You're making a mess of my convenience."

"I c-can't help it," the fat man released his grip and climbed down from the toilet seat. His feet splashed through the thick sea of sludgy shit as he moved toward Willy.

"Make me leave, you black bastard."

Willy screwed his feet and stepped back, threatening the fat man with his mop handle.

"Come on, hit me," the fat man bounded forward, covered in his own excrement. His hands dripped in the

Convenience

brown stuff. Each step he took kicked globules of crap into the air.

Willy backed-up and took several swipes at the fat guy. The fight entered the washbasin area.

Trey and Manny jumped in their shoes and backed up toward the urinals. They watched on in terror as the fat man, naked from the waist down, stepped like an ogre toward Willy.

"Stay away from me," Willy screamed as the mound of blubber crept toward him.

"Come here, dickhead."

Willy took a swipe at him. The end of the stick smashed him around the face. The fat man's head spun around and spat out a rope of blood into the ocean of shit behind him.

Willy looked up at the second cubicle. The sentence *I Know What You Did* was smeared across the tiles in dark brown diarrhea.

"Huh?" Willy shook his head and tried to focus on the writing. It was enough time for the fat man to take advantage and punch Willy in the face.

He tumbled back, his soles slipping across the brown sticky on the floor.

"Whoa," Manny shook his head as his veins ran thick with speed, "Trey, man, this is some good shit."

"You *don't* say," Trey yelped as he watched Willy scramble to his feet and hold the weapon up at the fat man. He turned to Willy and encouraged him to burst the blubbery creature threatening to kill him, "Take him down, man."

"I'm trying," Willy waved the stick at the fat mound of whale blubber stomping toward him. The lumpy jowls on the man bubbled and turned to liquid, drooling down his shirt.

"Gruuuughh," he reached up with his hands to his face and clawed away at the skin. Clumps of it came off under his fingernails as his head started to deflate like a withered old balloon.

Streams of blood spat out down his neck and dampened his shirt.

"What the hell is going on?" Willy screamed and took a swipe at his assailant. The end of the mop collided with the fat man's head. The wooden end went through it like a hot knife through butter. The man's head dropped into the sea of human waste behind him.

Trey turned to Manny, "I think we should leave, mate."

"Yeah. I like that idea."

They both made for the door.

Willy jabbed the beast in the stomach, sending it crashing shoulder blades-first into the sea of shit.

It writhed around and screamed in pain. Its stomach growled and began to inflate as the body rolled around in a pool of its own excrement.

"Shit, get out of here," Trey tanked the handle of the door down, "He's gonna *explode*."

The stomach grew and grew like a barrage balloon. Willy ran forward to the body and held the mop in the air like a dagger.

Trey and Manny couldn't open the door. The handle broke off and clanged against the ground, smashing a tile.

"Oh shit!" Manny turned around to see Willy about to stab the inflating stomach balloon.

Willy threw all his might down and speared the balloon with the end of the mop. It dug into the rubbery skin but didn't pierce it.

The belly retaliated against the strike and flung the handle into the air. The coarse metal object bopped Willy around the head. He dived to the floor and grabbed the wooden handle, sliding along the river of shit and fell to his knees.

He lifted the mop and stabbed the ugly beast in the belly once again. This time, it worked.

The stomach exploded, sending its large intestine and gore up and around the walls and ceiling of the gents toilet.

The defecation blast sent Willy crashing into the second cubicle, face-first into the diarrhea-filled bowl.

Trey and Manny looked up at the fat man's blown-out carcass. They too were covered in shit and guts.

"Gahh," Willy gasped, hanging over the toilet bowl. He spat a mouthful of shit to one side and gripped the side of the seat, trying to slide his knees back from the toilet.

He had no choice but to swallow some of it down. The place was utter carnage.

"You sick bastard," Manny screamed and splashed his way through the pool of watery shit toward the second cubicle. He side-stepped the man's engorged ribcage and moved behind Willy, "We're trapped in here. The door won't open."

Trey shouted from the front door, "How do we get out? I want to get out."

"I know," Manny kicked Willy's bent-over ass as he hung over the bowl, "Well? Answer me. How do we get out?"

Willy turned over his shoulder and shot Manny a look of death.

Manny wasn't pleased, standing behind him covered in the fat beast's waste, "Why are you looking at me like that?"

Willy smiled and scooped up a handful of stinking crap from the surface of the bowl and opened his mouth.

"Oh. No, no, no, no," Manny backed up and became furious, "You're not suggesting we *eat* our way out?"

Willy shoved his fist into his mouth and sucked off the fat man's excrement from his palm. He swallowed it down and let out a massive, deathly burp.

"You're sick," Manny yelled and rammed his fists together, "You're s o sick in the h-head."

"Manny, man," Trey screamed from the other end of the toilet, "What's going on in there?"

"The man's lost his mind," Manny shouted back, "Jesus H. Christ."

Willy shoveled another fistful diarrhea into his mouth, chewed through the lumpier segments and then swallowed them down. He smiled at Manny as the liquid brown mess drooled down his chin from his shit-smeared teeth.

"Okay, that's enough," Manny grabbed the back of Willy's shirt and threw him to his feet, "How do we get out of here?"

Willy grabbed the mop from the floor and took a swing at him. Manny took off his blazer in a furious rage and threw it to the floor, "Come on, dickhead. Hit me."

Willy swung the mop at Manny, forcing him out into the open gents area, "Get back."

"Come on," Manny held up his fists. Trey looked on as his colleague prepared himself to punch Willy's lights out.

"Manny, what are you doing?"

"I'mma knock this bastard's lights out once and for all."

"We gotta get to the board meeting, man," Trey screamed. "We're already ten minutes late."

"I know," Manny took a swipe at Willy's face and missed. Willy retaliated and swung the broom and smashed Manny across the face.

Blood fired from his nostrils, the majority of which hit Trey in the chest, "Ugh, Manny!" he cried like an agonized child.

Manny rolled his eyes and prepared to throw another punch. Willy jumped forward and whacked Manny around the head once again. Manny's head spun around 180 degrees and spat a tooth at Trey.

He caught it in his hands, "Manny, you're breaking apart."

"Get away from me!" Willy roared, preparing to take another swipe at his opponent.

Manny grabbed his chin with both hands, above his shoulder blades. He spun his head around and cracked it back into place - facing forward, "You broke my neck."

"You tried to attack me," Willy stepped forward as

Convenience

Manny moved back to the door.

"You deserve to die," his voice followed a few seconds after his lips moved, "Be careful you don't trip."

Willy listed the mop above his head, intending to bop Manny on the head and take him out of the game altogether.

"Come on," Manny squealed as he moved backwards, "*Hit me.*"

Willy screamed and shunted forward. He hadn't accounted for the fat man's carcass a couple of inches away from his feet.

Willy flew forward.

The ground lifted up in slow motion. The tiles on the ground careened with speed toward Willy's face.

He was falling over.

Mid-fall, Manny's fist flew into view in a vicious uppercut motion.

"Nooooo," Willy screamed as the second, third, and fourth knuckle on Manny's clenched fist connected with his forehead.

The impact was intense. Knuckles on Skull. It lifted Willy's entire body into the air and toward the long mirror above the washbasins.

His body flew back-first toward the mirror and smashed against it. The reflective surface streaked in all directions like an autistic spider's web. It pulverized as Willy's torso collided with it.

Willy roared as his body vanished into the darkness where the mirror once was.

Chapter 6

14:00 – 15:00

Darkness. Willy felt the cold, dank metal rustle up his back. He rolled over onto his side. The metal ground shunted down. It wasn't very thick. The action caused a rumbling noise shooting ahead of him.

It felt like he was in a tunnel.

He threw his hands out in front of his face. His knuckles hit another soft sheet of metal several inches above his head.

The sensation of claustrophobia was unsettling. He was surrounded by metal. A cool draft blew up his trouser legs. Something gnawed away at his ankles and scuttled around his feet.

Willy reached into his pocket and took out his lighter. He struck the flint a couple of times and eventually got a flame.

He could see that he was surrounded by four sheets of metal. Each wall shot in two directions, away from his head and feet. An endless metal coffin. The cold draught wafted past his face and threatened to put the flame out.

This was the air vent above the facilities. It was years since he'd been inside to fix the air conditioning unit. Even then, he never actually had to travel in the ventilation system itself. How he got here was anyone's guess.

The gnawing and scurrying around his foot didn't help matters. Lifting his head above his chest, he saw a little white tail disappear around the sole of his shoe.

He kicked forward, hoping to shoo whatever it was away from his feet.

From out of his trouser leg emerged a rat. Not any old creature, though. Willy knew it was the same rat he'd seen this morning -you could tell from its gaunt face and sorrowful eyes.

It squeaked and scurried up Willy's side.

"Oh God, not again," Willy huffed and laid his head down onto the cold metal sheet.

The tiny pitter-patter of the rat's footsteps raced through the tunnel as it arrived at Willy's face. Its nose wiggled. The rat investigated the blood splats on Willy's face and attempted to nibble on them.

"Would you knock it off," Willy whispered to the vermin. It took offense and backed off. The apologetic look on its face had Willy feeling sorry for it. "I'm sorry, little guy. I didn't mean—"

"Squeak," The rat showed its teeth and ran off down the vent, away from Willy's head.

The footsteps quietened down the further the rat made its way up the ventilation shaft.

Willy rolled over and tried to get into the prone position. His legs were the first to twist, followed by his waist. His upper body experienced a lot more pain.

"Aggghh," Willy yelped to himself as he shifted his chest toward the floor. The light flame knocked out, sending his surroundings into utter darkness once again.

Willy looked up and saw a small sift of light in the distance. The shadow of the rat fell against the side of the shaft. The shadow suggested the rat had grown ten times the size of the critter. It hadn't. It was just an optical illusion.

"Let's get out of here," Willy began to crawl toward the light at the end of the vent.

With each attempt to push his body forward, his elbows and knees producing a thudding metal sound. To minimize his presence in the vents, he'd have to crawl more carefully.

The rat had managed to reach the light blowing through the grill at the end of vent, before the left-hand corner.

"Yes, yes. I'm coming," Willy muttered. He took great care not to cause any more noise, he placed his elbow forward and hoisted his body along the metal surface.

Each movement caused Willy a considerable amount of pain. He winced and groaned as he felt his left arm buckle, sending him nipple-first to the metal.

"What was that noise?" echoed a woman's voice farther up the vent.

"I dunno," was the response from another woman.

"Anyway, you know that dude that cleans the toilets, here?" asked the first voice.

"Yeah, that lanky black fella?"

Willy screwed his face. There were two women having a conversation about him. Little did they know that he could hear everything. He kept moving as delicately as possible over the metal, careful not to apply too much weight on one limb.

The rat turned its head and made eyes at Willy. It extended its hand and pointed it down at the grill.

"They're talking about you, Willy," it said in an intensely high-pitch squeak.

"Who are they?" Willy shuffled forward with his elbows and reached the grill. Sifts of light bled through the five bars across the grill. They came from the ladies toilet. The vent opening looked down onto the cubicles from the corner of the ceiling.

"I dunno," the rat whispered back. "But they're definitely talking about you."

Willy threw his head over the bars and looked down,

"Lemme see."

The top-down view from the grill revealed two cubicles, with a woman in each one.

The first cubicle had a woman with red hair sitting on the toilet. She applied lipstick to her face as she relieved herself. A make-up box and mirror were firmly in her hand, enabling her to see what she was doing.

She ran the lipstick over her top lip, "Yeah, that guy."

"What?" the second lady asked, "Is he up to no good?"

"Something like that. I've heard he's been a very naughty boy."

Willy looked at the rat. It shrugged its shoulders and returned to looking down on the two women.

The second lady in the neighboring cubicle was a young blond. She had one leg perched on the toilet seat as she sat on it. She was inserting something between her legs.

"Ugh, these things are so difficult to aim on." She shifted her weight along the seat. Eventually, she hung her hand between her thighs and began to urinate. "Okay, I think I got it."

"Yeah, his name is Wally or something," said the redhead, mopping her brow with a cotton bud. Willy leaned down and noticed a skull-faced wedding ring on her fourth finger.

"Rumour is that he's a drug runner for the K-12 mafia or something. Keeps stashes of narcs hidden for his drug lords in his office."

"Really?" The blond woman said, holding the device under her thighs as she peed into the bowl. "So what?"

"So what?" the redhead banged on the cubicle wall and chuckled. "So, he's probably loaded. All we gotta do is steal it for ourselves."

Willy raised his eyebrows, "What the hell?"

"They've gotta be stopped," the rat whispered as he watched on through the grill in the vent, "Look over there."

Willy looked down through the bars and over to the

right-hand side of the room. A tall, leggy woman dressed in a bright red miniskirt and blouse was applying lipstick at the washbasins. The heels on her shoes were at least six inches. She could hear everything the two girls in the cubicle were talking about.

"We have to stop them, Willy," the rat said.

The blond woman tore off a sheet of tissue paper from the dispenser and wiped between her legs. She waved the little white device around in her hands, "Okay, here we go."

"Ohhh, how exciting!" said the redhead. "What are you hoping for?"

"I hope it says "just fat' on the readout when it works." She hit the flush and pulled up her jeans from around her ankles.

"Aww, you don't mean that," the redhead said from her cubicle.

The leggy woman in the red miniskirt dropped her make-up bag to the counter and let out a high exasperation. She turned around and leaned back against the basins.

"You do know everyone in here can hear what you're saying, don't you?"

"Eh? Are you talking to *me*?" said the redhead from behind the cubicle door, "Who is that?"

"Can you two keep it quiet in there?" said the leggy woman, who returned to the mirror, "You don't need to advertise your illegitimate schemes to the rest of the world, you know."

"Can you believe this bitch?" The redhead protested to her blond friend through the wall of the cubicles.

"Unbelievable," the blond woman yelled at her cubicle door. "You better leave these toilets now before I come out there and tear your wig off!"

"Pair of scumbags," the leggy woman muttered to herself.

"What did you just say?" the redhead asked as she

slipped her make-up pouch into her handbag, "You little whore?"

The rat scurried forward across the metal and looked down at the blond woman's hand. It lifted its head up to Willy, "They're going to rob you. We can't stay up here."

"They're going to rob me?"

"Yes, I have an idea," the rat moved forward and ran its face alongside Willy's hand, "Pick me up and lift the grill away. I'll distract them."

"Huh?"

"Just do it, you high-as-a-kite junkie man."

"Okay, okay," Willy unbolted the latches on the two near corners of the grill. The snapping sound against the metal caused the blond woman to look up and around, "What was that noise?"

"Shit, they've seen us!" The rat sat, perching over the edge of Willy's palm.

"I dunno." The redhead rose to her feet and pulled up her trousers to her waist, "Probably the pipes."

"Okay," the rat said. "Wait for it"

Willy carefully unbolted the two far corner latches from the grill. He lifted the square plate away from its enclosure.

The rat turned to Willy and prepared to launch out of his hand, "Drop me into the yellow-hair's toilet."

"Are you sure?"

"Yes, yes."

Willy extended his hand over the squared hole in the vent. The rat leaned back on its haunches and kicked its feet into Willy's little finger.

It sprung from his hand and plummeted forward into the blond woman's cubicle.

She looked at the little white pregnancy kit in her hand, waiting for the result to show, "Come on, come on."

The rat landed in her hand, next to the pregnancy kit. It looked up and smiled at her, "Hello."

"Agghh," screamed the blond woman, dropping the kit to the floor, "A rat. A rat."

She burst through the cubicle door and tumbled over onto the floor next to the washbasins, "Help me. Help me."

The leggy woman turned around and stepped back in disgust, "Ugh, what *are* you doing, you stupid blond tart?"

"There's a rat. It fell into my hand."

Willy saw his chance. He pulled himself over the man-size square opening in the ventilation shaft. He dropped his legs down through the hole.

His legs dangled from the ceiling over the second cubicle behind the leggy woman in the red miniskirt. He lowered the rest of his body through the shaft opening. He released his grip on the edge and dropped into the cubicle just as the redhead stormed out of the first one.

"What rat? What's going on?"

The blond staggered to her feet and brushed the long golden strands of hair away from her face, "There's a damn rat in here."

"A rat?"

"Yes," the blond squealed and pointed at the cubicles, "There it is."

The rat sat on its hind legs and wiggled its nose. The redhead froze, staring back at it. Neither of the three women could move.

"Jeez," the redhead stammered. "It's l-looking right at us."

The rat scurried over to the dropped pregnancy kit and pushed it forward with its little nose. It squeaked due to the sheer weight of the device.

"What's it doing?" asked the blond woman, petrified in her shoes.

"Seems it's found your pregnancy kit, mate," the leggy woman lifted her head from the basin counter and snorted a line of white powder.

The redhead and blond turned to her, only to realize that it wasn't a woman.

She was a transgendered woman. Male to female. Her

Adam's apple gave her away. She wasn't expecting the reaction she got from the two female friends. "What?"

"Ugh."

"Hey," the rat squealed in its high-pitch tone. It rubbed its nose across the pregnancy kit, "Do you know what the result says?"

The blond woman stepped forward and held out her hands, "No, no I don't. What does it say?"

The rat stood on its two back legs and held out its hands, "I'm going to be an uncle."

"What?" the redhead shrieked.

"It's blue," the rat chirped. "You're going to be a mommy."

The blond woman went for the rat. "You little bastard," she stomped her feet down, trying to squash it.

The rat sidestepped, a hair's breadth away from a crushing by the sole of her shoe.

"Come here," she screamed, chasing after the rat as it made for the ladies toilet entrance.

She launched herself into the air and stomped down once again. This time, she was successful. The sole of her shoe crushed the furry little creature to death.

A string of blood and guts spatted either side of her foot.

"Gotcha. You disgusting vermin."

Willy's phone beeped twice. A text message had come through.

All three woman turned their heads toward the second cubicle.

"Shit," Willy's voice came from behind the door.

"What was that beeping noise?"

"Shit, shit, shit," Willy remained perched on the toilet seat in the second cubicle. He took out his phone and inspected the screen. A text message had come in from Maxine.

Sorry about lunch, earlier. I'll drop by and see you at 6 pm.
Love, Maxine x

Willy slipped the phone into what he thought was his pocket. His hand rode against the side of his trousers. The phone missed his pocket completely as it left his grip and splashed into the toilet bowl.

"Bollocks."

The redhead walked forward. Her friend, the blond, had just emerged from the second cubicle. There was simply no way anyone else could have been in there.

"Who's in there?" The redheaded turned over her shoulder and looked at her friend, "The beeping came from inside there."

The redhead moved up to her and joined her in approaching the cubicle door, "I dunno, open the door."

The redhead thumped on the door. It was locked. The gap between the door and the frame didn't have the angle required to see who was inside.

"Open up. Come out."

No response.

Inside, Willy wiped his nose. A soft, white powder coughed up onto the side of his finger. He scrunched open his top lip and rubbed the substance across his gums.

The door thudded from the outside three times, "Come out of there!" the blond screamed.

Willy jumped off the toilet. His shoes hit the floor and didn't make a sound. He turned around and reached his arms into the toilet.

"Come outta there," the blond yelled once again, "Okay, enough. Let's beat the door down."

Willy dived head-first into the toilet. The rim of the ceramic bowl heaved out and swallowed the top half of his body.

The door banged violently from outside three times. The hinges rattled and shook loose.

One of them clanged to the floor.

"Hit it again," screamed the blond woman.

"I'm trying," screamed the redhead.

"Here, let me have a go," the leggy transgendered woman spat in her gruff, masculine voice. Her large feet clomped along the floor as the toilet gulped Willy's waist down into the u-bend.

"Stand back," the leggy transgendered woman yellow, "Here we go," she took a step back and threw herself at the door, feet-first.

The cubicle door blasted off its hinges and crashed against the flush. It knocked the lever on the flush down.

Willy's upturned feet shot down into the u-bend as the flushing water finished him off.

The transgendered woman held out her arms and turned back to the two ladies, "There's no-one in here."

"What?" the blond asked. "What do you mean there's no-one in there?"

"I heard a man say the word *shit*." the redhead added.

The leggy lady brushed down her miniskirt and stood aside, "Look, there's no-one in there."

The blond lady reached down and picked up the soaking wet pregnancy kit from the floor. Sure enough, it displayed a blue stripe.

She closed her eyes and took a deep breath, "Ugh, I must be going out of my goddamn mind."

The pipework behind the walls began to groan. The tiles on the walls rumbled. They fell, one by one, to the floor.

The blond woman rose to her feet in a state of panic. A mini earthquake was forming in the ladies toilet.

"What's happening?" she asked, afraid to look around the room. The intensity of the quaking forced the three women to lose their footing.

"Something wrong with the pipes?" the redhead yelled. "Quick, we better get out of here before the whole place falls apart."

The ground rumbled so viciously that the splattered remains of the rat jiggled around, streaking blood toward the washbasins.

"Right, let's get out of here!" the redhead screamed. She turned around and ran toward the door to the toilet.

The blond and redhead followed after her.

As all three women ran past the cubicles, a torrent of toilet water gushed from out of all six toilet bowls, splashing against the ceiling.

"My God," the redhead screamed. "Run. *Run.*"

The top of the room flooded rapidly. The water raced toward the open air vent in the ceiling and sucked into the metal tunnels.

The walls began to breathe and groan, shooting the tiles from the walls like mini bullets, crashing against the long mirror above the basins.

"Let's go," The redhead reached the door and yanked down on the handle. It wouldn't budge. "Shit. It won't open."

More tiles sprang from the walls. One particularly vicious jagged fragment pinged from the wall and stabbed the blond woman in the forehead. It killed her instantly.

"Oh holy Mary mother of God," screamed the transgendered woman, "Here, let me try."

"What the hell," the redhead raced over to her friend who lay dead across the basins. The jagged piece of tiling stuck in her forehead, spewing blood down the sink.

Parts of the mirror shattered sending razor-sharp fragments of glass all around her body.

The redhead stepped back and tried to keep her balance as the rumbling intensified. "Get that bloody door open!" She screamed at the transgendered woman.

"I'm trying, I'm trying. It won't budge."

She tried to step back, but her feet were engulfed by the spongy floor tiles. Each of them congealed together and crept up her long, soft legs. The woman looked down and shrieked for dear life.

"Help me. Help me."

The tiles doubled in length and crawled past her thighs. They circled around her waist, pulling her toward the ground. The rat's tail got caught in the swelling and rode up the side of her body. The tiles continued to smother her. They latched onward and up past her waist, turning her into stone.

"Oh G-God," the redhead screamed and backed away from the leggy lady, "Someone, *please*. Help us."

"Gwwuurrgghhhh," the leggy lady's body snapped in half at the spine. The tiles rolled out and latched across her face, suffocating her. Her body was being swallowed into the ground.

"Get me out of here. Please. Someone help me."

The entire length of the mirror smashed to pieces, revealing a deathly black nothingness above the washbasins. The blond corpse slithered from the deck and hit the floor, her wound fountaining blood across the broken tiles. Her eyes stared at her friend as she backed up, not knowing where to run.

The walls were closing in. The coffin that was the ladies toilet was getting smaller and smaller.

The redhead looked up to find the ceiling was closing down in on her. The walls scraped in from all four directions, causing a deafening grating sound. The concrete trailed its violent path toward the middle of the room.

"Help me. Help me."

The force from the jet of each toilet bowl was insane. A non-stop pummeling of toilet water flooded the ceiling as it projectile vomited from the toilet bowl.

The redhead tumbled toward the basins and landed against the wall. The room tilted sideways, causing her body to tumble onto the basins and tussle over the shattered mirror.

"Help. Help."

Before long, the entire room rocked around 180

degrees. The ceiling had become the floor.

The cubicles were on the ceiling, as were her two female friends. One of them had been stabbed to death. The other had been swallowed by the floor and settled amongst the ground's tiles, never to be seen or heard from again.

Blood seeped out from the lines that separated the tiles. The room began to fill with water as the walls closed in by the inch.

The swirling vortex created by the grill that Willy had jumped through was now drinking the contents of the room through its sharp bars.

The redhead was destined for a nasty death. The current carried her toward the grill feet-first. She held up her arms and tried to doggy paddle against the current. But it was no use. Her shoes slipped from her feet, then her dress tore from her body.

Her blouse was next to go.

Unclothed, she screamed her last as the water sucked her under and carried her toward the vent's grill.

Her toes jammed between each razor-sharp bar, tearing through the webbing in her feet.

The bone in her foot splintered apart and daggered out through her shin.

"Gwullscch," bubbles escaped her mouth as she let out the last of her oxygen.

The water flooding the ceiling-cum-floor raced around the strip lighting. It seeped into the electric housing. The bulb burst apart.

The organic matter in the water, including the two dead women and the rat's carcass, pulsed with blue streaks and smoldered due to the electric current. First, they'd been killed. Then, their bodies had been torched underwater.

The stench was unreal.

The water pushed the redhead's body through the sharp ventilation grill. The bars chewed through her calf and knee bone, snapping it in two and bending it backward. Her mangled, bloodied toes snapped up. They kicked into her waist as the grill tore up through her thigh and garroted her perineum.

A plume of blood bleached from her mouth into the water as she screamed. The grill diced through her body, effectively rendering her like a piece of meat being diced through a machine.

The water turned a dark red as her internal organs drifted away from her torn-apart body.

Her severed arms waded around, banging against the ventilation bars.

The redhead's face diced out like a chocolate orange in six, meaty segments.

The water rushed after her, acting as a final gulp of fluid to wash down the delicious meal. The flooding subsided and drained away.

The room let out a final burp and coughed the redhead's skull-faced wedding ring up to the ceiling. It clanged to the floor and rolled to a stop.

The room vibrated intensely once again. The water from the ceiling rushed toward the washbasins and crept up the ledge. The rest of it ran up the walls.

Then, the room began to rotate once again. The gravity caused the water - and the skull wedding ring - to roll up all four walls and head for the ventilation shaft opening.

For a moment, there was peace and tranquility. The notion of a job well done.

One of the taps started to groan and heave. The metal casing surrounding it bulged out. It seemed to want to vomit.

The tap waded left and right like a snake's head, trying to expel whatever was inside it.

A black man's hand shunted through the lips of the tap and felt around for something to latch on to. The basin was slippery. The tap heaved once again and puked out an entire black arm. The elbow chipped away at the chrome plating.

The hand grabbed the sill of the basin area and hoisted itself forward.

The tap groaned as its neck accommodated the man's head, which pushed through the hole. It was Willy, covered in liquid jelly. He gasped for air like his life depended on it.

Next out was his other arm. With both hands now on the edge of the basin, he was able to pull his entire body out through the hole at the end of the tap.

The unnatural sight of a grown man escaping from a small basin tap was insane. With a final hoist, he tumbled over the edge of the sill and crashed to the floor in a jellied heap.

He was naked and shivering, curled up in the fetal position.

"Ugh, ugh, ugh."

A final spew of clear jelly barfed from the tap and seemed to spit clear phlegm down the drain.

Willy's eyes snapped open. His buzzed, graying hair slicked back over his scalp.

He opened his eyes very slowly. The light grated over his retinas, causing him to cry like a little baby.

His right hand covered his eyes as he moved up to his knees. The slime roped off his arm as he extended it in front of his face.

Willy tried to speak. His voice came out like that of an infant learning his first words, "Ugghh, what h-happened?"

Willy cleared his throat and spat into the sink, "What," his voice deepened as he spat once again, clearing the detritus from his lungs.

"What," he said, in the same sentence, his voice grew back to normal, "H-Happened to me?"

He looked at himself in the fully restored mirror. He pressed the fleshy part of his index finger against his top lip. He was still missing one of his front teeth.

Willy hung his head. A dribble of slime slapped into the

bowl. There he was; a fully-grown nude man taking respite in the ladies toilet.

The door opened. Willy turned around to find an elderly lady with a gold earring and flowery shoes looking back at him.

She tutted to herself in complete disapproval.

"Tch. You should be ashamed of yourself," she complained. "Showing off your parts in the girls' convenience."

Willy turned to face the woman. She looked him up and then down. And kept staring *down*. Her attitude toward the situation changed once she saw what could be in store for her.

"On the other hand, maybe I could get used to the idea."

Willy shook his head, "Ugh, no. I'm sorry, I had an accident." He quickly moved toward the door and opened it.

"Oh, don't go," she licked her lips but realized that her chance had escaped her, "Well, you know where I am if you want me."

Willy only had to take twenty footsteps - past the vending machine and baby changing facilities - to reach his office door. All he had to do was cup his genitals in both hands and try not to slip on the jelly that drooped from his body.

He peeked around the corner to find the waiting area and benches opposite the vending machine teeming with families.

"Bugger."

Willy had no choice. He did what anyone else in his position surely would have done. He walked toward his office without a care in the world, as if fully-clothed.

He knew in his heart of hearts that as he walked past the mums and dads and boys and girls that they were staring at him. In a strange act of confidence he'd forgotten to cup his cock and balls.

How did he know?

The titters and chuckles - and resulting exclamations of horror - from shoppers of all ages rattled along the walls as he walked past them. How very embarrassing.

He reached the office door and pushed it open.

Chapter 7
15:00 – 16:00

Willy had changed into a fresh uniform. He'd managed to wipe away most of the gunk with a wet wipe. The fresh set of clothes weren't exactly *fresh*, though. Uncleaned since their last use, they stunk up a treat. That unmistakable stench of uncleanliness. Hardly the closest he'd ever been to God, by all accounts.

Willy looked up at the wall clock. 3:03 pm.

It had been a while since he visited the gents toilets. At least one hundred people must have been in and out during the course of the afternoon. There was no way it was in a respectable state, especially after the calamitous goings-on with the fat man an hour or so ago.

Willy grabbed Queenie in his right hand and exited the office. A smartly-dressed man came out from the gents toilet, zipping himself up.

"Good afternoon."

Willy nodded back at him as he moved past. He had meant to say "hello" but the way he was feeling didn't allow him to speak. His energy was better conserved for the clean-up job that lay behind the door to the gents.

Sure enough, the place was filthy. At least it was free from occupants.

Scraps of tissue paper lined the bank of the washbasins. Two of them had been left turned on and threatened to overflow over the lip of the basins.

"Tch," Willy muttered to himself. He moved to the basin nearest to the door and lifted up the handle. The water stopped spraying. This basic action seemed to cause Willy considerable pain. His armed ached. He caught his own wincing in the mirror above the tap.

Somehow, the day had taken it out of the poor guy. His face looked gaunt. Several lines and wrinkles streaked up his neck that he hadn't noticed before.

A quick check of his upper gum confirmed that his tooth was still missing. Of course, he knew all along that the tooth was absent. Every time he ran the tip of his tongue along the underside of his front teeth he could feel something missing.

He was used to that missing feeling. Only this time, it was physical.

The second tap stopped spewing water as Willy lifted it up. A new tap, a new mirror.

The same old ill-looking bastard stood before Willy. He reached up with his forefinger and peeled the bottom of his right eye down.

His eye was bloodshot. Had something got inside it? If it did then Willy wasn't able to recall what it was.

He noticed a small fly wriggling forward around the mirror. He snapped his fingers and tried to catch it.

Futile.

The little beast flew off and whizzed around his head as if taking the piss. Willy waved Queenie around in the vague hope that her head might catch it in mid-flight. It was no use. Willy had no choice in the matter. He'd have to attend to the next basin with that damn fly buzzing around his head.

Perhaps the fly had a point, he thought, as he scrubbed some yellow stains from the rim of the third basin. Flies generally only tend to hang around human waste. Shit, in other words. He thought it ironic, given the nature of his behaviour with his own daughter. With his wife. The fly was perfectly entitled to demonstrate what it thought about Willy as it floated erratically around his stupid, withered head.

It didn't help Willy's constitution, though. He felt like being sick into the fourth washbasin. Instead, he dry-heaved a treat. The top half of his body hulking up and out as if he was about to cough up both sets of lungs.

All he could manage was a clump of green phlegm into the plughole. A quick rinse under the tap would take care of that little mess.

"But Daddy, this toilet is for boys," a little girl said from behind Willy's shoulder. He turned around to find a bespectacled man in a tweed jacket walked a young girl of around four into the gents.

Willy and the man exchanged glances for a split second. The man knew where he was headed. The cubicles.

"Yes, honey," he pulled her forward, "But Daddy can't go into the girl toilets. He'll get funny looks."

"But, but—"

"—No buts, Chelsea," the man grabbed the door handle to the third cubicle, "Just get in and we'll do what we need to—"

"—But I don't need—"

"—Enough." the man pushed his spectacles up the bridge of his nose. He looked down at his daughter and walked her into the cubicle, "Let's get this over with. I don't wanna hear any complaining."

Willy shifted to the side and watched on as the cubicle door closed and locked shut.

The pipes along the wall fired up and groaned in what felt like slow motion. Then, the third toilet started to fire up and flush.

"Ugh, this is so disgusting."

Willy looked back in the mirror, examining his face. He didn't mean to eavesdrop on the happenings within the cubicle. Other than the pipework playing up, it was the only thing anyone could have heard.

"Okay, that's got rid of that nastiness," the man said. "Now, sit down."

Willy looked past the reflection of his shoulder in the mirror and pressed his hands onto the edge of the basin. It was cold and wet.

He could see the man's black shoes turn from their side to face the white bowl. The little girl's feet lifted up, suggesting she was on the toilet.

"C'mon, honey. There's a good girl."

Willy leaned over the sink and lowered his eyelid. Everything seemed fine until that zipping noise occurred.

Zip, zii-ii-ip.

"Shhh," the man said. "Come on. *Do it.*"

The girl went quiet. Willy sighed a pang of relief when he heard the tiniest of trickles hit the bowl. He grabbed Queenie and stepped with caution toward the cubicle area. Something had overwhelmed Willy.

The tinkling into the bowl stopped and was replaced by a light gurgling noise. Like someone squeezing the neck of a plastic bottle that was overflowing with soda.

The man caught his breath, "Are you done, sweetie?"

No response.

Willy put one foot in front of the other and eventually arrive a few feet opposite the third cubicle door. He made as little noise as possible.

"That's it, sweetie. That's it," the man's voice hushed.

Willy's face became puzzled. The "event" was over. All that needed to happen now was the obligatory wipe and flush, and they could leave. This was taking *way* longer than necessary.

Willy crouched down to his feet. His ass hung a few inches from the ground. He threw his head to the side to see the back of the man's shoes, a shoulder length apart.

The little girl's feet hung either side of the man's legs.

"Nearly got it, baby," the man seemed to wince, judging by the hastened sound of his voice. A small rubbing and sucking sound emitted from behind the door.

Willy realized what was going on. The groaning pipes seemed to confirm the sick, deranged goings-on within cubicle three.

Not here. Not in his facilities. No way.

Willy screwed his face and took one step forward. He clutched Queenie's handle in his right hand, determined to intervene.

Another step forward. Getting closer still to the door, the pipes seemed to gag and gurgle. Although he couldn't see them properly, he knew that the tiles were breathing in and out.

Then, just as Willy reached the door, the little girl coughed and spluttered.

"Ohh," the man groaned. "Now look what you've done, you silly girl."

"Sorry, Daddy," the girl's voice pleaded. "I don't feel too good."

"Ugh, you got it all down my trouser leg."

Willy bent his arm in front of his chest. It pained him to perform the action, but he had to break the door down. There was no time to unlock it, nor was there any time to lose.

Willy placed his left palm on the door and took a step back.

"Look," the man's voice came from behind the door, "Don't tell your mom, okay?"

"Okay."

A wave of sheer anger throttled Willy's body as he prepared himself to launch against the door.

"It'll be between us."

The flush sprang to life and the door opened. Shocked, Willy tripped forward on his feet and immediately stepped back.

The man stared back at Willy in surprise, "What are you doing?"

Willy looked at the urine stain splattered down the front of the man's trousers. He looked at the girl.

Untouched, fully-clothed and standing next to her father.

"Who the hell are you? Can't you see we're in here?"

"I'm sorry," Willy offered. "I thought—"

"—You thought *what?*" The man wiped down his trousers. His daughter had relieved herself successfully. Nothing untoward was evident whatsoever.

"I, uh, I work here," Willy scrambled for an excuse, "Do you need extra toilet rolls?"

The bullshit excuse didn't work. "What?" the man asked, extremely put-out.

"Sorry, I thought you needed some assistance."

"She had a slight accident, but nothing serious," the man eyed Willy up and down in return, "Were you *spying* on us?"

"No, no, I—"

"—I don't believe this," the man stormed forward, leaving his daughter to look up and watch in bewilderment, "Are you trying to say I was interfering with my own daughter?"

"No," Willy felt the man grab his shirt collar, "Not at all, I—"

"—Then what were you doing watching us?" the man blurted and spat in Willy's face, "You sick pervert."

Willy was about to retaliate but, instead, clutched his arm and wailed for dear life.

"What are you doing? Answer me," the man kept Willy up by his collar. He dropped Queenie to the floor. His body slunk in the man's hands.

"H-Help m-me."

Willy let out a death rattle in the man's arms. The little girl burst out crying.

"Let him go, Daddy. He's sick."

"Damn right he's sick," The man unhanded Willy. He crumpled to the floor in a heap of agony. His feet thrashed around as he clutched his chest. He found breathing extremely difficult.

The man looked on in pity as Willy writhed around in

turmoil.

"H-Help… *me*."

"Come on, sweetie," the man grabbed his daughter's hand, "He's obviously mental. Just ignore him."

"No, no—" Willy gasped and held out his hand to the man and his daughter. They ignored him and made their way to the gents door.

"I c-can't b-breathe."

The man gave Willy one final glance before he opened the door, "This place is as disgusting as you are. Tch."

He pushed the door forward, only to find that it wouldn't open. It was bolted shut.

"What the hell?"

The man rattled the door handle and tried to push forward, "It's stuck."

"Daddy, look," his daughter pointed to the washbasins. All six of them sprang to life, one by one, and blasted a constant stream of water into the plug. The noise was insane.

"What's going on, here," the man screamed and moved to the basins. The tap handles were all up. No matter how hard the man pushed down on them, they wouldn't relent. He got soaked to the bone in the process.

Each basin hastily overflowed. The water spilled over the edge of each basin and splashed against the floor.

Willy continued to scream and rolled over on his side, still clutching his chest. His breathing quickened. Both eyeballs started to bulge out of their sockets.

"Daddy," the girl screamed. "The black man. He's dying."

The man's shoes splashed across the floor toward his daughter, "Forget him, what about this water? We gotta get out of here."

Willy pointed at the cubicles. The last of them was still locked. Willy could see the stubborn shit creeping out of the bowl of the sixth cubicle.

The seats on the remaining five lifted up and banged

down over and over again on their respective bowls. The sound of hilarious cackling came from each one as the water from the basins flooded the floor. Several inches of water now filled the gents, threatening to completely envelop Willy's body. He thrashed around, spraying water everywhere, clutching his chest and trying to breathe.

"Daddy, why are the toilets laughing at us?"

"Oh my *G-God*," her father lifted her up into his arms, "Come on, Mister. We have to get out of here."

The man took long strides through the putrid water and sloshed over to Willy. He reached out to him with his free hand and discovered, much like Willy had done seconds ago, that the toilet seats were laughing at them. They acted like chattering teeth - slamming up and down against the flush handles and their bowls.

"Good God," the man gasped, failing to comprehend what was seeing. He grabbed Willy's hand and tried to hoist him to his feet. It was no good. Willy let go of the man's hand and grabbed at his own chest.

"I c-can't... b-breathe," Willy gasped as the flood rose up to his shoulders and over his body.

"Help, help," the father screamed, holding his girl's mouth in his hands to prevent her from screaming, "Shhh, honey, it's okay."

The girl roared into his mouth, ultra-scared that she was about to drown. She moved her head and continued to scream for dear life, "Daddy, the water is going bigger."

"I know, I know."

Willy slammed the back of his head against the tiled floor, cracking one of them. He split the back of his head open in the process. The blood from the cut smoked out into the water, turning it into a musky red and black ink.

"Whaarllb," Willy took his last gasp of oxygen whilst fighting his chest pains.

By now, the gents toilet was half flooded. The surface of the pool chest-high to a fully grown man.

Convenience

The man elevated his daughter in his arms above the water and waded toward the door to the gents.

The crystal clear water blasting from the taps turned into a putrid orangey-yellow. It jetted out even faster. The stench of gunky urine wafted around the room.

"Hold on, honey," the man reached the door and tried to kick it, hoping it would spring outward. The sheer weight of the water slowed the man's leg down as he tried to kick. It was absolutely useless.

The pungent, yellow water seeped through and clouded up the pool as it continued to rise up to the man's chin. He spat some out and lifted his daughter higher.

Turning around to the cubicles, he had hoped to find Willy swimming toward him.

It wasn't to be.

The man could just about see Willy's dead body wading in the urine pool. His arms stretched out and hung in front of his floating corpse.

Eventually, the man wasn't able to see any longer as the level the yellow water took his glasses away from his face. The man had no choice but to sink down as the room filled up.

His daughter dived into the murky water and thrashed her arms around. She rolled over in mid-swim and opened her eyes. Her little feet kicked her body forward, toward her father.

A burst of bubbles escaped from his mouth and nostrils as his final breath escaped his body.

"Daddy," she screamed. The oxygen from her lungs turned into a zillion bubbles of air that shot toward the ceiling.

Her father's body hulked forward. A streak of blood poured from his nostrils and mouth. His body slumped, dying in full view of his daughter.

"Noooo," she swam forward and tried to hug him. He was a clear ten feet away.

She didn't make it in time. Her last burst of oxygen

escaped from her lungs as quickly as his had done seconds before. Instead of taking in a lungful of fresh, clean air, she took in as much urine as her tiny lungs could accommodate.

The girl drowned. Dead in an instant. Her body relaxed, dead in the water. It floated toward her father's corpse. The pair of them knocked heads, sending her tiny body toward the door.

Willy's body floated in the middle of the pool. The gents toilets was now a final resting place. A *urinarium*. Three dead bodies expelled the last of their waste in amongst the putrid, yellow-green water.

The little girl's corpse knocked against the door. Willy's lifeless eyes happened to be facing her from a few feet behind. Her shoes drifted off her feet as the door opened, allowing the ocean of urine to flood through into the walkway.

The rush of water and pee flooded past the office and raced toward the shopping mall. The walkway quickly filled up with urine, allowing the three drowned corpses to drift out of the gents and into the waiting area.

The vending machine filled up with piss, soaking the contents. Further up the walkway, the elephant ride rattled on the spot. The *Twinkle Twinkle Little Star* song began to chime and bubble as it submerged in the water. everything in the walkway got engulfed in piss.

The father's corpse followed the girl's dead body past the vending machine. A few random shoppers who'd got caught in the flood tried to swim away.

One of them was wearing a red dress. She ran out of oxygen and died right beside Willy's dead, floating body. Her beautiful, long hair waded out from her head as her eyes turned into the back of her skull.

Alongside her, a bloated female corpse drifted toward the ladies toilet.

Eventually, Willy's head knocked against the office

door. His shirt collar became lodged between the door and its frame, suspending him in the center of the pool of piss.

Willy's head kept butting against the door frame. The jet from the washbasins kicked up a current that enabled the urine-laden water to travel down the walkway and flood the shopping mall.

But Willy wouldn't get that far.

His head knocked against the door once again. The urine escaped down his throat, adding weight to his body.

He began to drift downward. Sinking... lower and lower to the floor.

His lips got the handle and pushed down, causing the door to fly inward.

For a brief moment - as the water thundered into the office - Willy's face came alive. He gasped for air and quickly thrashed around in an attempt to shut the door and lock out the drowning pool.

The door shunted into the frame. Willy twisted the lock and wiped the piss from his eyes.

He was still in pain. Worse still, the pool seeped through the cracks in the door frame. It was relentless. Willy had about two minutes before the office suffered the same fate as the gents toilet.

The yellow water seeped under the crack of the door and quickly smothered the floor. Willy looked at the chair as it lifted a few centimeters from the ground and drifted away from the desk.

Willy didn't know what to do. He had no idea what to do with his final two minutes left alive.

It didn't seem to matter, as the pain in the chest and arm was getting the better of him. Willy wailed in agony and clutched under his left arm.

"Oh God, please. Help me."

He reached into his pocket with great anguish and took out his phone. He hit a button and pressed the device to his head, "Hello?"

"Hello?"

"I need help. I think I'm dying."

"Okay, sir," came the stern voice on the other end of the phone, "Can you tell me where you are?"

"In my office," Willy said, looking down at the water filling up the room past his knees. "Please, please. You must help me. I'm in so much pain."

"Yes, sir. Can you tell me what the pain is?"

"I haven't got time for th-that!"

"Please, sir?"

"It's a shooting pain. It feels like my— oh, God," Willy doubled over himself and squealed in agony.

"Sir, can you hear me?"

Yessss," Willy winced and sloshed around the room as it filled up to his stomach.

"Okay, listen. We'll get an ambulance out to you as soon as we can—"

"—Oh, God, please hurry," he wailed at the top of his lungs and felt around his midriff. The sensation of warm water rolled over the top of his hand, "I don't have long left."

"Okay. Can you give me your location, please, sir?"

"Yes," Willy coughed and squealed in pain down his chest, "Ugghhh."

"Sir?"

"Yes, it's the Kalei—"

Willy puked into the sea of urine flooding the office.

"Sir? Are you okay? Can you hear me?

Willy spewed again. This time, accompanying the green and yellow bile was a streak of blood.

"Sir?"

Willy coughed out the contents of his stomach from his mouth and tried to speak. The wall clock fell from the wall and splashed into the bloodied urine pool that was hovering around Willy's neck.

It read 3:50 pm.

"The Kaleido—schkoww."

"Sir, I can't hear you. Can you repeat, please?"

Willy dropped to his knees. The phone drifted from his hands as his body tumbled down into the piss pool.

"Hello," bubbled the phone as it bobbed around in the yellow pool, "Caller? Are you there?"

Willy watched as his phone bobbed toward the door. He was drowning.

Yet, he was in so much pain.

The last thing he saw was the picture of him and his wife and daughter as the water carried it away from the desktop.

The pain had to stop.

Willy was cocooned in a watery grave right in the middle of his office. The pain killed him before the urine-infested water did.

He took one last gulp into his lungs, knowing it would kill him - and knowing he had no other choice.

His lips opened wide. The buttons on his shirt broke off as his chest bulged out, taking in the last thing his lungs would ever receive.

His eyes widened as his chest exploded. A plume of dark red blood blasted its way through the orange-yellow pool of death.

Then, the bubbles of death escaped from every orifice in his head. Nose, mouth, eyes - even his ears.

Willy was dead.

Chapter 8
16:00 – 17:00

"Wha—" Willy snapped awake at his desk to find the office door being thumped repeatedly from the other side.

"Hello?"

Willy felt his forehead. It was soaked with water, as was the rest of his body. "Huh?" He rubbed his eyes and placed his hands on the tabletop. The place stank of urine.

A woman in a red dress ran into the room looking like she'd seen a ghost, "My God, quick, you gotta come and help her."

"Who?"

"There's a girl in the toilet, I think she's about to have a baby."

Willy jumped to his feet, "A baby?"

"Yes. Please, come quickly," the woman darted off to the right. Willy jumped to his feet and stopped the door from swinging shut.

"Hey, wait."

He ran toward the ladies toilet and kicked the sign to one side. He slid through the door to the ladies.

Six women gathered around the first cubicle, terrified out of their minds.

"Get out of the way," Willy yelled at them. They moved back to allow him to the cubicle door.

Sure enough, the woman with the blue hair was sat on the toilet, screaming and shouting. Her erratic breathing was beyond control. She placed her hand against each wall and kept her body still.

The heels of her shoes kicked around on the floor, pushing away some of the blood that had shot down her thighs.

"Help me," she gasped. "P-Please, help m-me,"

Willy dived forward. He wasn't an expert in these matters. "What do I do?" he quipped, trying to catch as much visual information as possible.

The blue-haired woman screamed again and threw him an evil look between her deep breaths.

"Do *something*."

Puzzled, Willy crouched down his feet in front of her and turned over his shoulder. The women looked at him, hoping he could rescue the situation.

"Aren't you going to help me?" he screamed at them. No, they weren't going to help. Willy was on his own. He had expected one or two of them to offer advice or assistance. For all the help they were providing, they may as well have just been a set of mannequins.

"What's your name?"

"Charlotte," she screamed, nearly booting Willy in the face.

"Okay, Charlotte," Willy held her knees in his hands and tried to push them apart, "I'm not a midwife. I've never done this before. I don't think you should be on the toilet for this."

"Shut up, you bastard," Charlotte threw her head back and as her breathing intensified, "Oh G-God, oh *G-God*."

"Just breathe," Willy roared. He tried to see the opening between her legs.

He turned around to the on-looking women once again. A couple of them had begun to cry. The rest looked on in wonderment, trying to predict what might happen next. One of them, a teenager, took out her phone and filmed the proceedings.

"We need to get her on the floor," Willy snapped and

squinted at the teenager's phone, "For Christ's sake, put that damn phone away. Can't you see this is an emergency?"

"You can't make me," the teenage brat quipped back, still holding her phone at him.

"She can't stay on the toilet, it's too dangerous—"

Charlotte screamed in a way that indicated that it was all over, "Yaaaooowwww."

Everyone's head turned to face her. A brief wave of silence fell across their faces.

"Yaaaooooowwww," Charlotte roared once again, "Oh God, oh God."

Two seconds later, a deathly "plop" noise occurred. Charlotte's legs wilted and slunk across the lips of the bowl.

She loosened their grip on the wall bars.

Her breathing slowed down. It was as if she was experiencing relief.

"Oh God, no."

Willy jumped to his feet and hooked Charlotte under his arms. He hoisted her to her feet and threw her against the silver flush on the wall. The small of her back threatened to snap on impact.

"Ugh."

"I can't see anything."

One of the women watching the scene screamed blue murder, "Holy shit."

"What is it?" Willy huffed as he kept Charlotte held up. He looked down but couldn't see anything. Her naked thighs and his trousers were blocking the view.

"Christ, keep her held up," screamed the woman as she darted into the cubicle, "Oh holy God, *no*."

The woman dropped to her knees and tried to grab at something between Charlotte's waist and the toilet bowl.

The sound of a baby's gargles bubbled up from the water. Willy closed his eyes, "Oh no, oh no—"

"—Hold her still," the woman screamed. She dropped

to her knees and reached into the toilet bowl, "Hold her."

A clanging sound shattered through the floor tiles from outside the cubicle area. Almighty thump and squealing followed after it.

"I am," Willy turned over his shoulder to see that the teenager had fainted. Her phone kept recording, pointing up at the strip lights on the ceiling.

The baby's cries turned to extreme agony. Even though Willy couldn't see it, it must have submerged into the bowl beneath the water's surface.

"I can't get it," screamed the woman by Willy's feet. She got up and threw her hands under the now-unconscious Charlotte's arms. "You try."

"Ugh, no."

The woman held Charlotte up against the wall, "Do it."

Willy took a step back and then crouched to his knees. As his body lowered, so, too, did the visual revelation of what had occurred a few moments ago.

A black and bloodied congealed rope hung from Charlotte's vagina, taut all the way down into the bowl.

Willy perched himself over the lip of the toilet seat. The fetus had become wedged under the water's surface. It flailed its tiny arms around, trying to fight its way to air.

"Oh, shit," Willy chewed down the urge to be sick and reached into the bowl with both hands.

The newborn threw its hands out, fighting for dear life. The jelly surrounding the body fused with the blood in the bowl, turning the water a strange purplish color.

"I can't hold her much longer," the woman cried from above Willy's head.

"I'm trying, I'm trying," he yelped back at her. He slid his fingers between the watery ceramic and the baby's body. He was making matters worse, thumping the side of its body further down.

"She's slipping."

"Keep her held up."

As Willy tried to cup the newborn's head, it screamed

Convenience

and kicked back. Finally, it opened its eyes. Willy was the first thing it saw as the dirty water bled across its retinas.

It kicked and gurgling, choking on the toilet water.

"Come on, come on," Willy muttered breathlessly to himself. He managed to slide his palm under the baby's head.

"Agh. It's n-no g-good," the women cried. Willy could feel Charlotte's body go limp. Her knees started to bend, indicating that the woman could no longer keep her held up.

At this moment, Charlotte's eyes opened. She let out a deafening scream and looked down at Willy's head.

"No. My baby, my baby."

"Keep standing,!" Willy yelled back, failing to grip anything other than the newborn's head as it cried for life.

"Ughhh," Charlotte's waist gave up the ghost, going limp in the woman's hand.

The umbilical cord stretched to a near-breaking point as the baby sunk further down the bowl and through Willy's fingers.

"I think I'm g-going to," Charlotte heaved and then dropped back against the wall. Her arse slid down, causing her thighs to push Willy's face back.

He looked up at her buttocks. They were inches away from the flush handle.

"No."

Her fleshy butt cheek sat down onto, enacting the flush. The screaming woman struggled to keep Charlotte up. Her body slipped through her hands.

The flush powered to life as Willy kicked back from the toilet bowl. The umbilical cord stretched even further and finally snapped, pinging flecks of blood and gore against Willy's face.

"My baby," Charlotte screamed as she looked down between her legs.

The newborn gargled its last, shooting down into the U bend and wedged sideways into the pipe.

The women watching behind them screamed and darted out of the toilet in tears. They couldn't bear to witness what they were seeing.

Willy wondered why the flush hadn't stopped. If anything, it continued its aggressive attack on Charlotte and her baby.

The water became more violent as the toilet gulped the newborn. The umbilical cord tugged away from inside Charlotte's groin, dragging her waist down to the toilet seat. It wouldn't snap.

The woman gasped, "Jesus Christ, it's going to take her."

All Willy and the woman could do was watch as the flush powered ten times harder, enacting its vengeance on Charlotte.

Gulp, gulp, gulp...

Down Charlotte went, crushing her limbs as they entered the u-bend. The umbilical cord hanging from her uterus dragged her down amid the flush. She was destined to join her newborn child.

"We need to cut the cord," the woman screamed, "It's killing her."

"Yaaaagghhh," Charlotte screamed amid the sound of breaking flesh.

"Christ alive," Willy screamed and pointed. Charlotte's head flipped back. Her mouth yawned open and vomited out a fountain of blood toward the ceiling.

At the same time, the yanking umbilical cord wrenched down into the angry flush.

Charlotte's legs kicked apart. Her uterus pushed through her vaginal lips, widening them across her inner thigh.

The blood she'd vomited came crashing down on her face. Her eyeballs sunk into her skull, collecting most of the gore she'd puked.

Her uterus splashed into the bowl and swirled around the insane flushing action. It just wouldn't stop.

The next to go in full view of Willy and the woman was Charlotte's stomach, from between her legs. Her buttocks ground down onto the flush handle, keeping it going.

"Grroooo," Charlotte screamed as her vital organs got sucked down into the bowl.

"I'll go and find someone," the woman hastened.

Willy agreed, "Yes, go and find someone. Anyone. Just go."

The woman left the ladies toilet as quick as she could, careful not to trip on the gore on the floor.

Willy rose to his feet. Charlotte had already been killed. The flush refused to stop its assault on her mangled, bloodied corpse.

Her stomach slapped into the bowl before her liver. Most of her internal organs got sucked down, causing her lifeless body to sink in on itself.

Before long, her legs and arms were next to go.

All Willy could do was stand and watch as the toilet ate her up. Her legs bent backward and folded against her chest. The toilet sucked her down arse-first, then feet and waist.

Her arms tiled up against the sides of her eyeless head. The last of her body - her chest and head - swirled around and around as the toilet finished its meal.

The flush powered on for a final swallow of her body, before calming down.

Then, the lid slammed to the bowl.

Blood, Wharton jelly, mucus, pee, and feces now formed the pool of spilled human waste swamping Willy's shoes.

The stench was beyond unbearable. It didn't seem to register on Willy's face, however. He closed the cubicle door out of respect.

Whatever needed to happen next could be dealt with by the police. Or a doctor.

Willy staggered out of the ladies toilets in something of

a daze - and caked in shit and blood,

Once again, everything played out in front of his eyes as if in slow motion. The clock above the baby changing room read 16:12. Less than two hours till the shift finished.

The office was the last place Willy wanted to be at this point in time. He just needed a quiet moment to reflect. It was just a matter of minutes until the woman who'd helped him with Charlotte returned with aid.

The facilities area was practically empty. The vending machine looked as pristine as ever. A child was riding the pink elephant.

"Everyone loves riding me," the childlike voice squealed alongside the irritating tune.

The baby changing facility seemed like an ideal place to take a breather. Only for a few moments before the inevitable post rush-hour commotion.

There'd be a lot of explaining to do, soon.

Willy pushed the door open with the side of his arm. He ducked his head. The light inside the facility was off. The door was thick enough to block out any commotion from outside.

The door closed behind him. He took a deep breath and ran his hands over his face. He didn't care that they were caked in nasty shit from the events of the past few minutes.

Finally. A moment of respite.

"Hey, what are you doing in here?" came a gruff man's voice.

Willy looked up in confusion. He reached for the light switch and pressed the button.

The lights snapped on to reveal a six-month-old baby standing naked on the fold-out table. Pale-skinned, and with a nasty scar across its neck, it looked very angry.

Moreover, the baby looked unreal. Standing on two legs, its back arched as it tried to step into a pair of tiny jeans.

"What?"

"What are you doing in here? Can't you see I'm changing?"

Willy looked the baby up and down. The rolls of fat on its arms weren't a surprise. The tiny nub of a penis pushed up by the waist of the tiny jeans. The baby seemed genuinely upset that he'd been caught *in flagrante*.

"I asked you, what are you doing in here? A bit of privacy would be nice?"

"Oh. I, er—"

The baby stepped into its jeans and buckled the belt, "Get out of here, you black *monster*."

"I'm sorry, I—"

"—Are you looking at my baby dick, you filthy monster?"

Willy looked confused. He shook his head, angrily. "No, it's just that I—"

"—Get out of here before I report you. *Monster*."

Willy swallowed and then put two and two together, "Did you, uh, just now?" he pointed toward the ladies toilet.

"Did I what?" The baby's voice deepened as it got angrier. It reached down for a tiddly t-shirt and threw it over his head.

"Were you just born a few minutes ago?" Willy tried, knowing full-well that his question sounded ever-so-slightly less preposterous than talking to a walking and talking baby.

"Nah, I don't think so," the baby rolled the t-shirt down its front, "Are you on drugs or something?"

"Well, no, I—" Willy's attention was caught by the black writing on it across the front of the baby's shirt.

I know what you did.

Willy's heart stopped.

The baby threw its hands open. He was very proud,

"How do I look, Willy?"

"Umm," he tried to speak with alarming difficulty, "You look... *good*?"

"Good. I'm glad you think so."

Willy didn't know how to respond, "Okay."

"Because you murdered me thirteen years ago."

Willy stood, defiant, "No, I didn't."

"Was it because I was white?"

"No."

"Oh, come off it, *Willy*," the baby crouched to its knees and sat on the edge of the fold-out changing bench. He pointed at his face and bare arms, "Look at me. Whiter than an albino. There was no way I was yours—"

"—But, I didn't k-kill you?"

"Yeah, you did," the baby said in its demonic growl. He traced his baby finger across his neck scar, "Twisted my neck and got rid of my body. Don't deny it."

"I d-didn't."

"You can spend the past thirteen years of your life convincing yourself it never happened," the baby said as he took out his retainer from his jeans pocket. He waved it around in his little fingers like a cigarette, "You can even lie to your wife that I went missing after you did it, but it was bound to catch up with her eventually. She was bound to figure it out, no?"

"No, no," Willy shook his head and tried to block out this apparition sitting before him, "It's all lies. You're not even real."

"Does Maxine know what you did?"

"No, she doesn't."

"Then you *admit* it."

"No, no. I didn't admit anything," Willy began to tear up as the baby climbed back to its feet. He threatened him with the retainer.

"Don't *lie* to me, Willy Gee!" He hurled the retainer at Willy's head, "You murdered me, you prick. You five-foot lump of festering shit-monster."

"Festering shit-monster?" Willy mouthed after him, "No, it's not true—"

"Where is that no good piece of shit?" A familiar man's voice came from behind the door. Both Willy and the baby turned to the frosted pane.

"Oh, shit," Willy gasped and looked at his wristwatch. It was twenty past four. He was late. "Ian."

"Willy," Ian's voice bellowed as he thumped the door to the office opposite the changing room, "Where are you, you wanker? Willy?"

Willy turned back to the baby, "I need to go—"

It had gone. No trace of its presence remained. The folded bench was securely locked into the wall. It always had been. Willy was now doubly sure of *that*.

He frowned and felt his body temperature rise, "I must be going mad."

Willy stepped out of the baby changing facility. He stood directly behind Ian, who kept knocking on the office door.

A man stood next to Ian - surly, and huge in size. All they had to do was turn around and they'd catch who they were after.

For a brief moment, Willy considered running down the walkway and out of the shopping mall altogether. It was the first of two options.

The second route would be to announce himself and get shot of Ian and his acquaintance quickly. Hopefully permanently.

As the knocking on the door continued, Willy weighed up the two options.

"I'm here," he said, causing Ian and his friend to turn around.

"There you are, my brudda," Ian threatened. "Ah been waiting here for twenty Goddamn minutes. Are you taking the piss or sumthin'?"

"Sorry, no," Willy said confidently and made toward

the office door. He took the keys out from his pocket and slipped the key into the lock. "Got held up, there was an emergency in the ladies."

Ian giggled to himself and nudged his friend in the ribs. "See Willy here, man? He's always up to sumthin', ya knaa."

"For real, for real," Ian's acquaintance said.

Willy unlocked the door. He felt Ian's hand on his shoulder. His fingers gripped around the bone, tightly, "See if you be late again, I'mma kill you. You embarrass me like that."

Willy closed his eyes and nodded, affirming that he understood Ian's threat.

Ian released his shoulder and pushed him through the open door, "Nah, nigger. Get yo' black ass in there. Let's do our "ting."

Willy set his keys down on the desk and crouched down in front of the safe.

Ian held his hand out to his friend, "Willy, man, this be Damien. He be my contact for the K-12 bruddas."

"Yah, man," Damien licked his teeth. "You got that 'ting for me, now?"

"Yeah, nigga," Ian watched Willy attend to the dial on the safe, "My boy, here, he safe. Kept it on the lowdown."

Willy spun the dial around.

The first number, one. The second number, one. The third number, eight.

But it didn't unbolt. Willy shook the handle and adjusted the numbers equidistant to each other.

"What's up, Willy?" Ian grew impatient and reached into his inside pocket. He grabbed hold of something, "You forgot the code or what?"

"No, no," Willy spat. "It's just that the safe is a bit temperamental. Hold on, let me try again."

Ian showed Damien a long, serrated knife. If he didn't get satisfaction, he'd be using it. Willy clocked the action in his periphery vision.

Little did the men know that Willy was trying to buy a bit of time. He was concerned that the parcels of *whatever* Ian had given him to look after might not be in the safe. He hadn't had a chance to check all afternoon.

Willy hoped it was time enough to formulate a plan. To get out. Hopefully, escape somewhere with his daughter and leave this godforsaken place once and for all.

As Ian and Damien grew evermore impatient, Will knew he was running out of time. He spun the dial around once again.

One, one… *eight*.

Finally, the lock clicked open, sending the door springing toward his knees, "Got it."

Willy stood to his feet and pulled the rucksack out from the safe. He set it on the table and pointed toward the open door, "It's in there."

"I know it is," Ian felt his patience being tested. "What? You not gonna get it out?"

"My back hurts. Can you do it?"

Ian frowned and passed the blade to Damien, "Tch. 'Low a nigger, man."

Willy grabbed the picture of his wife and daughter and placed it face down on the desktop. Neither of the two men saw him do it - they were far too preoccupied with the safe.

"It's all there, man," Willy offered as he sneakily crept toward the door, eying the handle, "No-one's touched it."

"They better not, man. It better be here." Ian hitched up his trouser legs and crouched down. He reached into the safe very slowly. Damien fiddled with the knife and kept an eye on Ian as he poked around.

"Where is it? I can't see shit?"

"Right at the back," Willy took hold of the office door handle, "You have to reach *right* in."

Damien turned his head to Ian as he reached further into the safe, "I can't feel nothing?"

"What?" Damien blurted. "What do you mean there's nothing in there?"

"*Shit*," Willy yanked the door handle down and pulled the door back. He made his escape from the office.

Damien caught his shirt collar and yanked him back into the room, "Where the *hell* do you think you're going?"

Damien booted the door shut and smacked Willy around the face. He was incandescent with rage.

Ian held his phone up to the safe and switched on its torch mode. His face fell when he realized that there was nothing inside it.

"Assholes," Ian screamed and slammed the safe door shut.

Willy trembled in his shoes. This was it. Ian and Damien were going to carve him up into several pieces. They'd be doing him a favor.

Ian jumped over to Willy grabbed him by the shirt collar. He licked his lips and tilted his head. He had a dead serious look on his face, "Where's my 'tings, motherfucker?"

"I d-don't know."

"What ya mean ya don't know?" Ian spat in Willy's face. A glob of phlegm ran down his cheek. "I'mma ask *one time*, nigger. Where is my 'ting at?"

"I d-don't know. I checked earlier and it was—"

"—I swear to *God*. Y'all make a nigger ask one more time, I'mma slit your throat…"

Willy blinked and slipped his hand around Queenie's neck. Ian shifted aside, keeping hold of Willy as Damien lifted the knife and placed it at his throat.

"See my boy, Damien?"

Willy nodded.

"He gonna puncture your damn neck meat, dig it around. Make it painful. I ask one more time, where my 'ting at—"

Willy kicked Ian in the stomach, sending him ass-first against the safe.

Convenience

"Shit. Ian, man," Damien screamed.

Willy head-butted Damien on the nose. The blade cut across Willy's throat as he performed the action. It was enough to send Damien back, wailing through the blood shooting from his nostrils.

Willy lifted Queenie and smacked Damien in the face with the mop end.

"Get that prick," Ian screamed as he climbed to his feet.

Willy burst through the office door with Queenie in hand.

A stream of shoppers barreled down the walkway and blocked Willy's escape. For the first time in the convenience's entire history, everyone and his mother needed to use the toilet at the exact same time.

Willy had no choice. He looked back and saw the office door burst in. Ian and Damien were seconds away. He turned to his left and made for the gents toilets.

Willy ran over to the door and slipped on a wet patch. He almost lost his balance, but Queenie kept him up as he perched himself against the wall.

Ian ran through the office door and into the walkway. Damien barged past him and waved the knife around, "Where'd that bastard go?"

The shoppers screamed and turned around. The sight of a nasty, hulking beast of a man wielding a knife was enough to frighten them off.

Willy pushed through the gents door, alerting his two assailants.

"Over there. He's over there," Damien screamed and ran after him.

Willy entered the gents toilets. He had a quick decision to make. Two men were at the urinals relieving themselves. They turned to look at him.

"Get out of here, now."

The two men chuckled to themselves and turned down to their waists, continuing to pee.

"I mean it."

Still, they wouldn't respond. Willy thought of an idea, "There's a fire in the building. Get out now."

The man laughed harder, treating the announcement as a joke.

Willy stepped back and wedged his foot against the gents door. The pane of glass blackened as Damien and Ian made their way and tried to barge in.

They were unsuccessful. Willy's foot kept them out, but wouldn't do so for much longer. All it took was a decent enough barge from one of the two giants and the door would push Willy onto his ass.

"Help me," Willy screamed at the men, "The door, the door."

One of them men zipped up and walked over to Willy. The door banged inward every few seconds.

"Willy, man," screamed Ian. "We know you're in there."

"What's going on?" the man asked. "Who are they?"

"Oh, uh," Willy thought on his feet. "They're here to fix the pipes. The door's stuck, can you hold it?"

"Okay."

"Put your foot there. Between the floor and the door."

The man did as instructed.

Willy stepped back toward the cubicles, keeping Queenie tight in his grip, "Keep that door shut. There's flooding on the other side."

"Willy, you're a dead *nig*," screamed Ian from the other side of the door.

The other man at the urinal turned around and watched the commotion. He was unaware that he was peeing all over the floor.

Willy backed himself up by the cubicles. They were all empty, apart from the sixth one.

Damien yelled at the door from the other side, "We're

coming in and we're gonna kill you, Willy Gee."

The man at the door started to complain, "Um, I don't think the door will hold—"

The door slammed inward, sending the man's face crashing against the washbasins.

Ian and Damien stormed in and looked around. They saw an unconscious man's body sprawled out across the washbasins. The other man continued to pee, his penis hanging through his trousers and his hands in the air.

Ian and Damien eyed the man up and down as he continued to surrender and relieve himself at the same time.

Ian snatched the blade from Damien's hand, "Where'd he go?"

The man stopped peeing. A few droplets of urine fell from the tip of his dick and splashed against the floor. He pointed toward the cubicles.

"What, in there?" Damien asked.

The man nodded, "Yes," and kept his hands up.

"Get out of here, we're not after you," Ian smirked to himself as the man raced out of the gents, "Yo, you might wanna zip up before you go out there."

A few gasps could be heard from the walkway. Some of the shoppers hadn't expected to see what they saw. A grown man running away from the gents with his penis hanging from his zipper.

The door shut behind Ian as he turned around and watched Damien boot open the first cubicle.

"We know you're in here, Willy," Ian stepped forward scratching the sharp end of the knife across his thumb. He licked his lips and saw Damien step out of the first cubicle.

"Ain't in here."

"Try the next one," Ian paced toward the cubicles, "Come out, Willy."

Damien booted the second cubicle door off its hinges, "Come out now, Willy Gee, Willy Gee."

He ran into the second cubicle. No-one.

"He ain't in here, either."

"Shit, Damien, man. Check them all," Ian ran up to the third cubicle and took a step back, "You're dead, Willy Gee."

Ian booted the third cubicle door off its hinges.

Willy perched like a bird on the toilet seat in the fifth cubicle. He held Queenie across his knees, as he felt the fourth cubicle door bust apart.

He stood up straight and peered over the gap between the fourth and fifth cubicle.

He saw the top of Damien's balding head as he surveyed the interior, "Not here, brah. That just leaves the last two."

"Willy," Ian said as Damien ran out of the fourth cubicle, "This is it, nigga. Moment of truth."

Willy closed his eyes and muttered something under his breath. He gripped Queenie in both hands like a baseball bat.

Willy opened his eyes and stared at the cubicle door, "Come and get me."

"You heard the man," Ian screamed. "*Do it.*"

The fifth cubicle door burst off its hinges. Damien ran in and found no-one.

Unbeknown to Damien and Ian, Willy had climbed over the tiny gap and into the sixth, locked cubicle.

He fell down to his feet. The sound indicated that someone was indeed in the sixth and final cubicle.

"Right, the last one," Damien yelled.

Ian thumped against the sixth cubicle door, "Shit."

Willy looked down at the toilet bowl. The stubborn turd that had been there all day had grown to five feet in size. Much of its body trailed out of the pan and tailed off along the floor.

It seemed to be breathing. The midsection of the substance blew out and then back in.

"What the hell?" Willy whispered to himself.

The door smashed inward, slamming against the wall,

catching the tip of the five-foot turd.

Willy screamed in pain and grabbed his ankle. Damien and Ian stared at Willy and smiled.

"You're gonna hurt so bad, man, I swear," Damien growled, marching forward with the knife.

Willy jumped to his feet and whacked Damien in the stomach with Queenie's head.

"Oooof!" Damien flew back into his friend's arms.

Ian shoved him aside and stormed into the sixth cubicle and swiped at Willy with the knife.

The blade caught him across the throat. Several jets of blood sprayed out from Willy's neck.

"See what happens? When you mess me around?"

Willy shoved the fat, bottom end of Queenie into Ian's stomach. The force sent him tumbling back.

"No!" Willy attempted to scream through his gaping, slit throat, "Grroowllscchhh."

"That damn nigga's out of his tiny ickle mind!" Ian ran back into the cubicle and stabbed Willy in the gut. As he yanked the blade out, a part of Willy's liver jutted out of the wound.

Willy slipped back and landed against the wall. He caught sight of the elongated turd.

The top fifth of it had been slit and bled a yucky brown substance. It appeared to have been stabbed two feet down its body. The stab wound released some white fragments of embedded food.

The stench was rotten. Ian could barely withstand it as he crouched down and pointed the blade at Willy.

"See this, here?" Ian scolded Willy. "This is where you die."

Ian stabbed Willy in the chest, directly into his heart. The five-foot turd bled from a slit one-third of the way up.

Willy coughed out a clump of ultra-dark blood. He loosened his grip on Queenie. The mop clanged to the floor.

His eyes rolled to the back of his skull. Willy died in

front of Ian and Damien.

Justice had been served.

"Don't deserve to live." Ian sighed and felt Willy's neck for a pulse. "No good piece of shit."

"Is he dead?"

"Yah, man," Ian turned over his shoulder. "Schooled the hard way, man."

"What do we do with the body?"

"We leave it here, innit?" Ian said to Damien. "Let some next man clean this shit up."

Damien's face was wrought with terror as he looked over Ian's shoulder at the floor. He pointed at Willy's body.

"What is it, man?" Ian asked.

"Look, look."

What Ian saw forced him to instinctively kick back along the ground in a state of near-paralysis, "Jesus Christ! What is *that*?"

Chapter 9

17:00 – 18:00

Ian kicked his body along the floor with his feet. His heels skidded on the wet ground. He slid backward and out of the sixth cubicle.

He covered his mouth with his right hand and pointed at Willy's juddering body, "Oh, Holy Mary mother of God."

Damien stepped back alongside Ian, stunned, "This is an abomination, brah."

Willy's corpse heaved at the waist as the fat end of the elongated turd punched its way into Willy's mouth. Like a giant effluent rattlesnake, its body shimmied from top to bottom and shunted itself into Willy's throat. It burrowed down into his stomach.

Willy's body convulsed with each punching motion that the fat, long streak of shit inflicted.

Ian climbed to his feet and backed against the wall. "Wh-what's happening to him?"

"I dunno, but I don't wanna stay to find out," Damien barked. "Allow it, man. Shut the door and trap it."

Ian walked forward and grabbed the edge of the door and yanked it shut. The plan didn't go well. The door had been kicked off its hinges and fell onto the giant turd, causing it to shriek.

The door crashed to the floor. The hinges scraped along the wall and buried themselves into the slimy, brown substance.

"Oh *dear*," Ian took a couple of steps back and watched the remaining half of the turd slither its way into Willy's body. His top lip folded like a condom over the top of his head, exposing his flesh and skull.

Willy's stomach inflated as the excrement slopped down his throat, through to his chest and inside his body.

Damien puked on the floor. The smell was beyond tolerable. Ian grabbed him by the shoulders and tried to shift him away from the cubicles. Damien dropped to his knees and planted his fists on the floor.

"We gotta get outta here, brah," Ian screamed at Damien. He was convinced that they should leave Willy to suffer his attack alone.

Damien vomited once again, spraying puke along the tiled floor and soaking Willy's shoes, "I c-can't m-move," Damien squealed with a mouthful of spew.

Ian looked at the monstrosity on the floor. The tail-end of the turd finally heaved itself through Willy's mouth. His lips met in front his mouth.

A sliver of excrement ran down his face and slapped to the floor.

"Damien, brah. That's it. Let's go," Ian pointed to the door. He clocked the unconscious man lying across the washbasins slide down to the floor.

A deathly growling noise came from Willy's newly-formed body. It kicked around. Willy sat up straight and puked a torrent of bloodied shit down his shirt.

"Grrassshhh," Willy's lips waved across his face. His eyeballs flipped around and faced Ian and Damien.

The two men froze solid and stared at Willy for his next move.

"Willy, man?" Ian tried, softly, so as not to upset the corpse, "You okay?"

Willy hopped to his feet in one fell swoop. The motion was about as unnatural as physics would allow. What happened next confirmed to Ian and Damien that pursuing Willy further wasn't the best course of action.

Ian squinted at Willy. The skin on his face bleached and bubbled down his shoulders, burning through his shirt. The seams on his sleeves split open and burnt up as they hit the floor.

Willy's ribcage rustled through the skin on his chest, revealing his internal organs. His lungs liquefied in front of Ian and Damien's eyes. They turned to mush and slopped down the front of his trousers, burning the material.

Anyone else witnessing this perversion of science would have run a mile by now. But not Ian and Damien. They couldn't help but look in wonderment.

As Willy's clothes smoked around his ankles, the rest of his human body cracked open like a shell. It split apart, revealing a thick, double-over shit monster.

A large basketball-sized clump of brown gunk rose from between his legs. As the ball reached its summit - eight foot above its feet - the shit-monster fully formed.

It snarled at the two men, revealing a row of sharp teeth.

Two six-foot limbs jutted out from its waist resembling whips.

Two five-foot stumps for legs and a complicated spider web arrangement of nubs acting as toes.

The creature stepped forward. The tiled ground cracked under the sheer weight of the eight-foot creature.

"W-Willy?" Ian held out his hands in self-defense, "Is th-that you?"

The creature surveyed the two men and rolled its shoulders. The beast stank of crap. Long streaks of droppings slopped down to the floor.

The creature hulked its body and roared at them, sending specks of shit in their direction.

Damien darted over to the washbasins. The creature slapped one of its two heavy, shit-tarred arm-whips at Ian.

He let out a prolonged scream. The creature paused for a moment and looked at Ian. A line of blood scored its way from his left ear, across his cheeks and nose, to his right.

Ian's crying stopped. The top half of his head slid away from the bottom half, bounced off his shoulder and smashed against the floor. The impact caused a lot of the contents of his skull to scatter messily over the floor.

"Ian, man," Damien turned around and made for the door. He tripped over the unconscious man's body and fell nose-first to the wet tiles.

Three of his teeth dislodged themselves from his upper gum. The force of his head hitting the ground was enough to discombobulate him.

Damien flipped over to his back and kicked himself toward the door, "No, no."

The shit creature moved forward. Such was its size, each step seemed to be staccato as it thumped against the ground. It caused mini earthquake in the room with each stomp of its foot.

Damien kicked his feet at the monster, trying to reach up and grab the handle of the gents door. Only the unconscious man lay between him and his assailant.

"Get away from me," Damien yelled at the top of his lungs through his shattered upper palate. He spat some blood at the shit creature, but it was futile.

The creature stomped forward once again and extended its whip-like arms. A towering, eight-foot shit monster loomed over Damien. It threatened to take him out of the game - permanently. It let out a loud fart-curdling, crap-laden roar of utter turmoil.

The whip limb scooped the unconscious man around the knees and lifted it into the air. The man's head whipped up and hit the ceiling light, shattering the bulb and cracking the ceiling. The creature swung the man's body around and around, threatening to attack Damien.

He rose to his feet and held out his hands, "Somebody, help me. Help."

The creature twirled the man around, gripping him by

his knees.

Damien was about to scream his last but wasn't given the chance. The side of the unconscious man's head whirled around and thumped the side of Damien's. He flew into the air and crashed, back-first, against the mirror hanging over the basins.

Sharp fragments of metal and glass howled around him and daggered into his body.

The creature held the unconscious man's body in both whips and lifted him into the air. It let out a God-like scream and lifted its right knee.

Damien watched as the creature slammed the man's lower back onto its knee, splitting the body in two.

"Ahhh, shit. Shit," Damien barreled over the central washbasin and covered his face. "P-Please d-don't kill m-me."

The creature held the two ends of the man in its clutches. It looked over to Ian's body and turned back to Damien. Its left hand pointed at Damien with the lower, severed half of the body in its grip.

"Nooo," Damien cried one last time.

The creature clobbered Damien with the lower half of the man's body, followed by the upper half in his other hand.

Bang, bang, bang, bang! The beats wouldn't stop. A giant, violent smash on Damien's face and body like two baseball bats.

Both halves of the man's body broke apart as it collided with Damien's. Flesh and whatever organs remained flew into the air.

The gents toilet turned red and yellow with all the human detritus and gore splattered around it.

Thud, thud, thud.

The fifth body blow was the one that killed Damien. The hip bone of the human battering ram puncture his eye and pierced deep into his brain.

The creature dropped the two ends of the human

baseball bat to the floor and turned to face the door.

"Ladies and gentlemen, welcome to the Kaleidoscope," announced the speaker system in the southern perimeter walkway, "Today is late night shopping."

The door to the gents toilets blasted off its hinges and crashed its way along the walkway. Several shoppers making their way toward the convenience area jumped in fright. They turned around and ran back toward the stores.

The eight-foot shit creature seemed to have gained height - and a vicious, brown tail. It clambered forward, tucking its chin down to its chest.

Two of the shoppers screamed and ran off in the opposite direction. A pregnant woman tripped over the waiter's bench and hit the floor stomach-first.

The creature bounded forward and barged past the vending machine. It tipped it onto its side, crushing the woman under its sheer weight. A splat of blood streaked from either side of the carnage.

"The Kaleidoscope will be open until eight o'clock this evening," the announcement came as the monster pushed forward.

At the far end of the walkway, Ted clutched a set of papers under his arm. He looked at the creature bounded toward him, "What the hell is that?" he screamed to anyone who would listen.

The creature scraped the side walls with its arms as it paced forward on its path of destruction. It tilted its head at the pink elephant ride.

"Everyone loves to ride me!" it said, despite not being in operation. There was no child sitting on top of it.

It sprang to life and bounced back and forth, playing its tinny *Twinkle Twinkle Little Star* music.

Ted backed up and spun around on his feet. He screamed at the shoppers outside *TriMarque*, "Everyone, get out of here. Now."

They didn't listen to him and went about their slow,

casual business.

"Can't you hear me?" he asked. A few of them looked at him like he was mad. He took a deep breath and decided to announce something else that might make them move.

"Fire. *Fire.* Get out of here, now."

His exclamation worked. The shoppers picked up their pace. Most of them became curious and peeked around into the walkway.

They discovered a ten-foot monster made of shit punching at the walls. Waving its claw around, it stormed toward the main shopping area.

"Oh my God," one of them screamed and ran as fast as she could toward the Kaleidoscope entrance.

Ted jumped into the middle of the concourse and held out his hands. He waved the set of papers at them, "Everyone out. There's an emergency. Go, go, go."

The shoppers hurried in all directions. Some of the children with them wailed as their parents lifted them into their arms and ran off.

"What's going on, here?" an elderly man asked Ted.

He pointed at the walkway - and the approaching commotion. The elderly man's face fell, "Oh, shit."

They were joined by a security guard who'd seen the commotion, "What the hell is—"

He caught a glimpse of the creature booting the vending machine up the walkway. The plug dislodged from the socket and sparked as the device screeched toward them.

"What the hell is that?" the security guard screamed at Ted.

"I don't know. But we have to get out of here."

The security guard took out his radio, "This is Mike. I repeat, this is Mike," he said as the creature battered everything in sight. It was half-crushed in by the ceiling and walls, trying to break free.

"We need *everyone* down at the southern perimeter. Past the fountain. Right *now.*"

"Shouldn't we call the police?"

"I am, I am," the security guard spat and took out his phone, "We need all units down at the southern perimeter of the Kaleidoscope."

Ted rolled up his papers, clutched them in his fist and turned to the security guard, "Seal off the entrance. Have everyone head up to the northern area. Now."

The creature reached the elephant ride and went to grab it. The bright blue painted eyes on the elephant's face focused on the creature, "Don't hit me."

The creature kept his arm raised and tilted its head. The elephant crawled off its platform and flapped its huge, plastic ears.

"Everyone loves riding me," it giggled in its child-like voice. The elephant turned around on its feet and offered the creature its behind. Its tiny tail whipped around, pointing at the saddle. "Do you want to ride me?"

The creature shuffled forward. Its shoulders smeared shit along the top half of the two walls. It grunted and threw its right leg forward, spilling effluence in all directions.

It tried to lower itself on the elephant's saddle. The toy ride giggled to itself and shunted forward a few feet, causing the creature to fall to its knees.

"Haha. Fooled you," the elephant raced forward and flapped its ears. Like Dumbo, it launched a few inches into the air and hovered in front of the creature.

A section of the creature's knee broke free, resulting in a lump of crap splatting to the floor. It roared in pain between its teeth.

"You're gonna have to do a lot better than that if you want to kill me, Daddy." The elephant's right eye winked at the creature. It floated backward, paving the way to the shopping mall, "You wanna kill me?"

The creature stood back up, using each of the walls as balance. Its whip-like arms smeared manure across the tiles as it finally stood back up and marched forward, after the elephant.

"That's it, big boy. That's it. Come, fly with me," the elephant turned around, flapped its ears and flew towards the shops.

"Run, run," Ted screamed at the shoppers. The creature dived out of the walkway and slammed against the *TriMarque* store font, causing the windows to explode.

It roared and flung out its arms. Since consuming Willy's body, it seemed to be growing exponentially. Its neck and mouth extended out, gnashing its teeth at the shoppers. The beast was at least fifteen-foot high and dripping with diarrhoea, most of which collected up around its feet.

Ted ran backward with the security guard. He stopped to take in the sheer size of the monstrosity towering over them, "My God…"

The security guard grabbed Ted by the shoulder and tried to get him to move, "No time to stop. Let's go."

The elderly man looked up at the fifteen-foot tower of shit and dropped his jaw, "My, oh my. You *are* are a big beast, aren't you, son?"

The creature looked down at the man and scooped him up by the waist with its shit tentacle. It flung its arm back and launched the elderly man into the air.

His body hurtled across the concourse and crashed through the *Bean There, Done That* glass window, setting off the security alarm.

Rose hopped over the information desk and ran over to Ted outside the CD store, "What's going on?"

"I don't know," Ted said. "But it's tearing the place up."

"What do we do?"

"We get out of here before it kills us."

Ted, Rose, and the security guard slowly backed up.

They watched as the creature punched the first level landing, shaking the groundwork to the core. A few shoppers fell over the edge of the landing and hit the lower deck, breaking their bones in the process.

"Everyone get out of here," Ted screamed at the remaining shoppers on the first level, "*Now.*"

They all ran as fast as they could in the opposite direction.

The creature elbowed the hanging lights, bursting the bulbs and continued its destruction. It swiped at the pink elephant flying around.

"You'll never catch me." It's body buzzed around inconsistently in front of the creature's face, "Come on, big boy."

The elephant wasn't visible to Ted, Rose and the security guard. The latter took out his radio and held it to his face, "Guys, where are you?"

"We'll be there in thirty seconds."

"Hurry up." The radio fell out of the security guard's hand.

Rose turned to Ted and looked at the papers in his hand, "Where's Willy?"

"I don't know," Ted said, turning around and spotting the flaming lantern. "I haven't seen him since the police were here."

"The police were here?" Rose looked on at the creature as it smashed another shop window. The shopping mall was quickly turning into a wasteland.

The shit beast turned around, trying to snatch the flying elephant out of the air. To the guys on the ground, it looked as if the monster was having an epileptic fit.

"What's it doing now?" Ted screamed, trying to keep up the creatures aberrant behavior.

"It's trying to catch something," Rose muttered.

The flying elephant buzzed around, egging the creature to catch it.

"See you outside, Willy," it chuckled and flapped its

way toward the Kaleidoscope's southern perimeter doors.

It vanished through them in a puff of purple smoke.

"Christ. *Willy*," Ted turned to Rose, "He's still there. Someone better get Willy out of the conveniences."

"Willy," Rose screamed and looked around, "Willy, are you here?"

She noticed a pair of arms reaching through the *Bean There, Done That* storefront. Shattered glass streaked out across the ground.

"Help me. Help me," came a voice from within.

Rose stepped forward, "Jeffrey? Is that you?"

"Yes, yes, help me!" he screamed. "I'm badly hurt."

"Rose, no," Ted yelled after her as she hopped over toward the smashed glass.

"He's hurt," Rose shouted over her shoulder and crunched her way through the glass.

The creature smashed its head against the upper deck, decimating the first level decking. The ground smashed away on impact, streaking through the fecal remains of its head.

Rose held out her palm, "Quick, Jeffrey. Grab my hand."

He grabbed onto her hand and lifted himself to his feet, "Thanks. What the hell is that thing?"

"Rose," Ted yelled. "Get him out of there, now."

She looked up at the ceiling. The back of the creature bubbled away, coughing up long ropes of blackened shit to the floor.

A suitcase-size glob of crap splashed to the ground, next to Rose's leg, "I don't know, but I don't want to stick around to find out."

"Jesus Christ," she yelped and pulled Jeffrey toward her, "Ted."

"What?"

"Look at it," she roared. "It's melting! The damn thing is falling apart."

Jeffrey looked up and puked into the air, "Gahhh."

"I know. It stinks, doesn't it?"

Rose and Jeffrey ran, hand in hand, away from the creature just as it spotted them moving. It lifted its gargantuan foot of poop and stomped down, behind them, missing them by a few millimeters. The wave of splattered shit hit their backs, propelling them forward.

The beast let out a God almighty roar and threw its arms onto the first level and tried to hoist itself up to the ceiling. Its feet flailed around as it tried to dig its dirty soles against the storefront in an attempt to ascend to the next level.

"What's it doing?" Jeffrey wiped the puke from his lips, "My God, the stench is gut-wrenching."

"It's trying to climb," Rose looked up in awe at it, "I think it wants to get out."

The creature lost its balance, piercing its foot through a jagged window pane. It puncturing through the crap and lacerated the creature's foot. It wailed in pain and stumbled back, falling into the information desk.

Two security guards came from the north end of the shops and couldn't believe what they had seen.

"My desk," Rose cried. "It's destroying my office."

"If it wants out, then let's help it," Ted offered.

"No," the security guard interjected as the rest of his team joined from behind, "Stop. Think for a minute. Imagine what would happen if that *thing* got out into the open?"

"We can't have it in here." Ted turned to the lantern and looked at his papers.

"Ted, man," the security guard said. "What are you doing?"

"I'm going to solve this problem."

He ran over to the lantern and rolled the papers into a tight, protruding club. The end of it shot into the open flame and caught alight.

Ted turned around and waved the fire stick at the creature, "Hey, shit head. Over here."

"Ted, what are you doing?" Jeffrey spat, fearing for his life.

The creature spun around and looked at the flaming end of Ted's papers. It scrunched its shit face and growled at him.

Ted carefully moved in front of the information desk with the makeshift torchlight held above his head. He lowered it and set the wooden beams on fire, creating a barbecue in the middle of the shopping mall.

Ted kept moving with the flames in his hand. The creature twisted with him, seemingly afraid of the fire.

"That's right, that's right," Ted headed to the entrance as the beast turned to him, "Let's take this outside, asshole."

The monster growled. As its face and mouth bent, long ropes of diarrhea slapped to the ground beside Ted.

"Ted," Jeffrey screamed. "what are you doing?"

"I want this piece of shit out of my mall."

The creature let out a crap-laden roar as Ted threw the papers at the Kaleidoscope doors.

The ball of fire smashed through the window and rolled to a stop by the fountain.

"Quick, let's go," Ted hollered as he ran through shattered door windows.

Jeffrey, Rose and the three security guards ran after him.

The creature couldn't stand to be near the fireball that was the information desk. It examined its arm. A touch, hardened skin formed over the length of it. The heat caused its body to stiffen in the spot.

"Go, go," Ted screamed at the others as they raced through the carnage.

The creature stomped down in agony. Rose and Jeffrey changed direction. They darted between the creature's dripping legs and headed for the smashed door.

Outside, several children were shooting each other with

water pistols. They'd filled their guns with the water from the fountain.

Two dozen shoppers were milling around on their phones by the doors.

A ball of fire smashed through one of the doors to the entrance to the mall. The glass pushed through and scattered to the ground.

It rolled to a stop a few feet away from them.

The shoppers outside yelped and backed up. "Bomb. Bomb," one of them screamed.

The sound of the creature groaning from within the Kaleidoscope frightened everyone into action. They backed away from the benches and intended to run off to safety. Curiosity got the better of them. They hung around to watch what was happening.

Ted ran through the broken glass and shooed everyone away, "Get back. Get back."

"What's going on in there?"

The quickest way to get everyone away from the chaos was to lie, "There's a bomb."

"A bomb?" One of the shoppers repeated. That particular word made all but a few shoppers run for the hills.

The kids dropped their water guns to the floor as their mums and dads picked them up under their arms.

"We gotta go," a concerned mother said. She took her son by the hand and marched him toward the road.

Jeffrey and Rose ran through the smashed glass and out into the front of the store.

All four sets of double doors pounded as the creature kicked at them. One set of windows exploded, followed by the second set.

"Shit," screamed one of the shoppers and backed up, "What's going on in there."

"Help us," screamed one of the security guards from behind the doors, "We're stu—"

An almighty crunching noise throttled around the

doors. The security guard's head rolled forward onto the patio, covered in excrement.

Ted ran over to Rose and Jeffrey just as several police cars pulled up in front of the building, "Oh, thank God."

The exterior of the building crumbled in front of a huge smashing noise. Parts of the brickwork flaked out and dropped to the floor.

Ted turned around and watched as the creature took another strike at the building. Its contours were barely visible through the battered frontage.

A deafening boom rattled from within the mall. The hulk of a creature squealed and pummeled the front from within.

"It's trying to get out!" Rose said, "the fire must be upsetting it!"

Jeffrey looked over Rose's shoulder. He saw several armed officers hop out of a police van. The rest of the officers exited their cars and approached the front of the building.

"Okay. Everyone get back."

An officer with a megaphone perched himself over the roof of his vehicle, "Everyone, stay back."

The monster stepped back and ran forward with its head out front. It battered the front of the Kaleidoscope, smashing entire facade to pieces. Sharp bits of debris fell around the officers and Ted, Rose, and Jeffrey.

"What is *that*?" the officer screamed as he looked up at the creature. Thousands of flies had taken an interest in it and buzzed around, trying to pick away at its head and shoulders.

The creature's excrement body hardened. Its arms and body were now fully-formed. An enormous twenty-foot-high abomination made of human waste. It shifted the sharp detritus from the floor and roared a rasp of shit spittle at everyone below it.

Jeffrey stepped forward and waved his hands at the beast, "*Hey*. Over here."

Rose darted after him and tried to grab his shoulders, "Jeffrey, no. What are you doing?"

"Trying to catch its attention," Jeffrey he said as he moved to the benches. He climbed on top of them and jumped in the air, waving his hands, "Over here."

The monster swung its head, spraying excrement left, right, and center. It focused its gaze on Jeffrey's swaying arms.

Rose backed up and took a look at the beast, "Jeffrey, no."

"Come and get me, you big mound of shit."

"Okay," screamed the officer with the megaphone, "Take aim and fire at will."

"Yessir," another officer affirmed. He aimed his rifle at the creature. The rest of the officers cocked their rifles and took aim at its head.

The creature swiped down with its huge arm and grabbed Jeffrey around the waist. It stomped toward the fountain, keeping its excretion-ridden claws around Jeffrey's legs.

He looked the creature dead in the face, "My God, you stink."

The creature clenched its other claw around Jeffrey's waist. It had the poor guy in both hands.

"Go to Hell," Jeffrey spat into the creature's face.

"No, Jeffrey."

The creature snapped the man's spine and pulled him in two. Jeffrey's internal organs splashed out and slapped against the ground. In one fell swoop, the creature flung the two halves of his body into the air.

"That's enough!" The chief of police roared into his megaphone, "Fire."

The officers fired a round of bullets at the creature. Bits of the creature exploded as the bullets pinged off its body. Flecks and wedges of crap sprang into the air as it moved forward, waving its hands around.

"Kill it," Rose said. "Tear that bastard to shreds."

The creature was visibly hurt from the incessant bullet hits. It stumbled forward and dropped to its knees in front of the fountain.

"Cease fire!" The chief of police held the megaphone to his lips.

The gunfire had caused the flies to burst into flames around the monster's head. From a distance, it looked like the flamed flies were creating a halo effect around the roaring beast.

"Cease fire, damn it."

The top-half of Jeffrey's body splatted to the ground, right by the chief's feet.

"Gah," he kicked the spongy organs away from him, nearly slipping on the torn-out pair of lungs in the process, "Christ, that's disgusting. Get this cleared up."

The fountain water seeped into the beast's legs and began to break it apart. It grabbed a hold of the five-pronged stone star at the top of the fountain.

"It's slowing down," one of the officers said. "Look."

The fountain spray jetted into the body and head of the beast, breaking down its consistency. As it held on for dear life, parts of it broke off and slopped into the fountain below.

The creature let out a roar of deathly pain as the water eroded its body. Its torso softened and began to putrefy against the jet of water.

Several streams attacked it from all directions, puncturing large holes in its body. The beast's body broke away in sections. The shitty remains sloped down its legs and mixed in with the pool of water wading around its knees.

"My God. It's killing him," Rose screamed.

Three huge chunks of shit fell into the fountain, dissolving into the swirls of water in the stone moat.

The beast rested its forehead on the star. The sharp end daggered between its eyes, causing the wound to cough out a torrent of diarrhea down the stony structure.

Rose raised her eyebrows and noticed something in its mouth. It cried to itself, slowly breaking apart into the fountain.

A small front tooth slipped forward through its sharp teeth. It fell toward the floor.

Rose stepped forward and caught the ivory object in her palm. She opened her fingers out.

One white, front tooth stared back up at her from her palm. She looked up at the creature's dissolving face, "*Willy?*"

The creature lowered its head, before a stream of water cut through its neck and severed it completely.

It wedged between the beast's body and stonework, before splashing down into the flooded moat.

Ted joined Rose to watch the monster vaporise into the fountain water.

"What did you set fire to back there, Ted?" she asked, smearing some the congealed feces away from her forehead.

"The southern perimeter plans."

The front of the building would surely need redesigning, anyway. This end of the Kaleidoscope wasn't fit for any kind of purpose.

The entire front had been destroyed beyond repair. The fountain would need an extensive and thorough cleaning.

The stores at the southern perimeter - including Rose's information kiosk - would need a complete overhaul, too.

The entire building looked exhumed. Flames and fire chewed away whatever was left of it from within.

A tear rolled down Rose's cheek as she watched the last of the creature's body wither away to nothing in the vortex of water. The fountain had consumed the beast.

She turned to Ted and tried for a smile. But it was no good.

It was over.

***

5:50 pm. Maxine approached the *Kaleidoscope*. Nothing was unusual about it. No damage had been done. Everything was perfect.

A man tried to enter the shopping mall but was blocked by the security guard.

"Sorry, sir. We're closing for the day now," the guard said, patiently.

"But, it's ten to six," the man protested. "There's another six minutes."

"Sorry, we're closing early. Come back tomorrow."

The man turned around in anger and stormed off, "Late night shopping my ass."

Several shoppers with bags of groceries and other items exited the doors and made their way home. It was dark by now and the mall was closing for the day.

A security guard held the door open for a couple, "Have a lovely night."

"What's happening down there by at the toilets?" the woman asked.

"Oh, it's nothing. There was an incident a while ago," the security guard said with a smile, "Nothing to be concerned about."

The woman accepted the answer and walked away with her partner. Maxine sprinted to the door just as the security guard closed it.

"Hey, wait."

"Sorry, madam. We're closing early today."

"No, no," she placed her foot in the path of the door preventing the guard from shutting it.

"Please, madam."

"No, you don't understand," she quipped. "My Dad works here. I'm just meeting him to take him home."

"Your Dad?"

"Yes."

"Oh," the guard pushed the door open with concern, "Who's your Dad?"

"He works in the convenience. Just down that walkway, there."

She peered through the door. A few people were milling around halfway down the entrance to the public toilets, "Can I come in?"

"Yes, okay," the guard allowed her through, "If anyone asks you were already in."

She walked insistently toward the corridor leading to the facilities.

A policeman was arguing with Ian and Damien in front of the elephant ride. He prevented them from getting any closer to the toilets.

"I'm sorry, but you'll have to come back tomorrow once the place has been secured."

"But he's my friend. I want to see him," Ian threatened. Damien didn't look very pleased and folded his arms, "Man, just let us in. He has something that belongs to us."

"Oh, really?" the officer quipped. "What is it? I can go in and see if it's there?"

Ian turned to Damien and raised his eyebrows, "Oh, uh—"

"—Tell me what it is."

Maxine walked past them, briefly making eye contact. They didn't know each other. She saw a few more officials outside the office chattering among each other. A cordon had been put up in front of them advising pedestrians to avoid the area.

"What the hell?" Maxine muttered to herself.

"Excuse me madam," another officer stood in her way and held out his arms, "I'm afraid this area is out of bounds for the moment—"

"—But I'm—"

"—There's another convenience you can use at the north end. I'm afraid you can't—"

"—No, no," Maxine explained. "I'm meeting my father, he works here. I'm taking him for his check-up."

"*Your* father?" the officer said, at once taking a

different, more solemn tact with her.

"Yes, his name is William. He's the janitor here."

The officer looked at Maxine and frowned, "Okay, okay. Can you wait here just one second for me?"

"What's going on? Has something happened?"

"No, hold on," the office whispered and up to the office door. Maxine looked back up the walkway to see Ian and Damien walk off. They seemed angry.

She took a step forward and made eye contact with a man in a suit who came out of the office. He took the stethoscope from around his neck and joined the officer.

"Can someone tell me what's going on, please?" Maxine asked, fearing the worst.

Seconds later, the doctor and the officer walked Maxine into the office.

Willy sat in his chair, dead. The top half of his body sprawled sideways on the desk. A framed picture of his family lay face-down a few inches from his fingertips.

He was dead.

"Dad," Maxine bit her lip and walk around the table. She looked at the doctor, "What happened?"

"I'm afraid he passed away, Miss Gee."

"When?"

"We're not sure. We got the call forty-five minutes ago. We arrived about five-thirty," the doctor stepped in front of the shaken and upset Maxine, "I've notified the coroner. He's on his way, now."

"How long ago did it happen?"

"That'll be all, thank you," the doctor said. The officer exited the office and stood in the doorway.

"Taking everything into account, he's been dead for about a couple of hours, now."

"A couple of hours?" Maxine became enraged, "Why are you here now and not two hours ago?"

"As I say, we weren't actually notified until half an hour ago. I and the first responders came as quick as we could."

Maxine sat on the chair, opposite her father. She stared at his lifeless face. His tongue was out and his eyes were dry, staring at the wall.

"He was very ill," Maxine said through her tears.

The doctor tried his best to console he,. "Yes, I know. We don't suspect any foul play. Although there were a couple of men a few moments ago who were very insistent that they needed to come in."

"Who were they?"

"It doesn't matter," the doctor said. "They seemed interested in the safe, of all things. One of the officers asked them for the code, but they didn't know what it was."

"The safe?" Maxine asked.

"Yes," the doctor nodded at the lock, "but it's not priority right now. The coroner will conduct the post-mortem and as the safe isn't company property, all his belongings will go to his next of kin."

Maxine stood up and wiped her eyes, "Do you mind if I have a moment or two?"

The doctor smiled politely and made for the door, "Yes, of course. I'll come back in a couple of minutes."

"Thank you, doctor."

He left the office, leaving Maxine alone with her dead father. She stepped over to his body and ran her fingers through his hair. She closed her eyes, trying not to make a nuisance of herself.

Maxine walked over to the safe and crouched down in front of it. She didn't know her father had a safe. All she could see was the ability to open it with three digits.

She closed her eyes and twiddled with the dial. Then, a revelation. The birth date of her deceased sibling.

January 18th.

She spun the numbers around to read one, one, eight on the lock.

The door opened inward. It took Maxine by surprise. It made her cry properly, this time.

All these years - thirteen of them - and no-one had ever mentioned her little brother, or why he died. Yet, his date of birth was clearly still on her father's mind.

She pushed her arm into the safe and felt around. Something plastic. She grabbed one of them and pulled out a wrapped parcel.

Maxine wasn't stupid - she knew what it was, "Christ, there must be at least twenty thousand pounds worth, here," she muttered.

The parcel went back into the safe. As she was about to close the door, she noticed a small piece of paper taped to the inside of the door.

She tore it off and unfolded it. A note from her father. Maxine read the note. As she read, the drops of tears turned to floods. She couldn't control her quivering lips.

Maxine, if you're reading this, then I am dead. I didn't have the guts to tell you the truth. It's true, I did kill your little brother. I couldn't stand the thought of him not being my own flesh and blood. I have been dying for months. Inside and out. I know what I did and am riddled with guilt. I'm sorry. I love you. Dad.

"Everything okay?" the doctor asked from the office door.

Maxine swallowed, folded the note and looked up at him. Yes, yes. Everything's fine. Thanks."

"We're going to have to ask you to step out as the coroner's just arrived."

"Oh, sure," Maxine shut the safe door and spun the dial around. She took one last glance at her father as the doctor and coroner moved into the room. She leaned down gave him one last peck on the cheek.

"I forgive you."

She turned and smiled at the doctor as best she could, "Oh, can I ask?"

"Yes?"

"If those guys come back, they're lying. They're only

after my father's stuff. Please tell the authorities that they're not to interfere, here."

"Oh, certainly," the doctor said as the coroner attended to the corpse, "I'm not his doctor. But I'll let his doctor know."

"If anyone asks, I'd rather they not know about any next of kin," Maxine added and made her way to the door.

"Don't worry, it's not our business to inform strangers about others' affairs."

"Great. Thanks."

The doctor smiled as she exited the office.

Maxine thanked the officers in the walkway for their time. As she headed for the entrance of the immaculate Kaleidoscope mall she could hear an argument in full flow. Ian and Damien were in a verbal battle behind the doors.

She smiled as she recognized the tinny jazz version of one of her father's favorite tracks. *Save Your Kisses For Me* by The Brotherhood of Man. She whistled to herself as she made her way to the double doors.

The security guard allowed her through and wished her a pleasant evening.

She couldn't help but hear Damien threaten the morose-looking Ian as she made her way to the main road.

"When I'mma meant to get your shit back, man?" Ian protested. "The place is crawling with doctors and filth, brah."

Damien wasn't happy. If anything, he was downright apoplectic, "Oh. Whenever's bloody *convenient*!" The response was soaked in sarcasm.

Ian ducked his head in shame. He knew he was in serious trouble.

"I swear to God, you fat bastard," Damien yelled into Ian's face, "You better get my shit back or you're dead. You hear me? *Dead*."

"Yeah, man," Ian muttered, afraid for his life, "I hear ya, brah."

"And don't call me *brah*," Damien smacked Ian around the head, "You useless piece of shit."

A smile crept across Maxine's face.

The guard was right. It may have been dark and cold, but this evening may turn out to be a pleasant one, after all.

Acknowledgments

For K
Also to:
My immediate family
The CVB Gang Members / ARC Street Team
Jo Huber, who's just a wonderful PA. But she's mine, so lay off!
The members and admins of 20BooksTo50K
Adele Embrey for her invaluable razor-sharp eye
My stalker Jennifer Long for all the usual reasons,
and a few naughty ones.
And to all the public toilet janitors in the world…
this is sort of for you.

*Check out **PURE DARK** and **GLITCH** next…*

Get Your Free Short Horror Story!

Subscribe to the
Chrome Valley Books mailing list!

TO KILL A PREDATOR

ANDREW MACKAY

Just type the link below in your internet browser!

bit.ly/ToKillAPredator

If you liked Convenience...

You'll love the **Pure Dark** series.

Set inside the coma of a heroin junkie, these short horror stories will make you question your own sanity!

It's the ultimate horror endurance test.

Go on, take the challenge.

We dare you.

bit.ly/PureDarkSeries

If THE SKULL appears on your device... *DO NOT TOUCH IT.*

*Get your copy of the terrifying cyberpunk horror novel **now**.*

mybook.to/glitch

About the author

Andrew Mackay is an author, screenwriter and film critic. A former teacher, Andrew writes in multiple genres: satire, crime, horror, romantic thrillers and sci-fi.

His passions include daydreaming, storytelling, smoking, caffeine, and writing about himself in the third person.

A word from the author

I hope you enjoyed this book. Please check out my other books at Amazon and remember to follow me there.

If you enjoyed the book, please leave a review online at Amazon US, UK and Goodreads. Reviews are integral for authors and I would dearly appreciate it.

I love to engage directly with my readers. Please get in touch with me - I look forward to hearing from you. ***Happy reading!***

Email: *andrew@chromevalleybooks.com*

NOTE: If you purchased this title at Amazon, then you can download the e-book version for **FREE** with Kindle Matchbook. The last pages of the e-book version contains exclusive author notes and behind-the-scenes material for each title. It's a real treat for fans, so *download it now*! ☺